Taking Art to Heart
The Life and Times of A.Z. Kruse

Self-portrait. 1928. (Lithograph).

Preparing the Sabbath. (Woodcut).

Taking Art to Heart
The Life and Times of A.Z. Kruse

A Biography by
Benedict Kruse

Edited by
Bettijune Kruse

Northwest Publishing, Inc.
Salt Lake City, Utah

Taking Art to Heart: The Life and Times of A.Z. Kruse

For information address: Northwest Publishing, Inc.
6906 South 300 West, Salt Lake City, Utah 84047
JC 08 31 94
Edited by S. J. Davis

PRINTING HISTORY
First Printing 1994

ISBN: 1-56901-054-4

NPI books are published by Northwest Publishing, Incorporated,
6906 South 300 West, Salt Lake City, Utah 84047.
The name "NPI" and the "NPI" logo are trademarks belonging to
Northwest Publishing, Incorporated.

PRINTED IN THE UNITED STATES OF AMERICA.
10 9 8 7 6 5 4 3 2 1

To Liane, Martin, and Steven
for the joy they have brought to the lives of their grandparents and parents
and whose lives testify to the aesthetic integrity lived and espoused
by their grandfather, Alexander Z. Kruse.

Street Musicians. (Lithograph).

Table of Contents

Treasure Hunt. (Oil, 20"x16").

Foreword

Anyone who has even a passing interest in twentieth century American art should read this book. The reason is that in learning about Alexander Kruse, one will also glean a good deal about the amazingly diverse New York art community in which he was inextricably involved. Regardless of the level of one's knowledge of American art of the first half of this century, the reader will find fascinating material (including plenty of anecdotes) about an artist-critic and his friends. That about Alexander Kruse which has hitherto been unpublished comes from a reliable source, Benedict Kruse, who not only observed his father in his studio, but actually witnessed many of the conversations and events presented here.

But if Alex Kruse's participation in the art community of the first half of the twentieth century is relatively important, why do we not know more about him? The answer to this question is that his kind of imagery fell out of fashion. He began making pictures under the spell of Robert Henri's realist group, the Ash Can School, and he refused to depart from representational subjects at a time when abstract imagery all but eclipsed the older mode. Alex Kruse had the distinct advantage (or an observer in

1960 might have seen it as a disadvantage) of knowing and studying with progressive masters of unvarnished realism in American genre. He learned from them that the hugely popular style of impressionism was more French than American and, therefore, derivative. He learned that just because a scene was not pretty, it was still not only worthy of an artist's interpretation, but frequently more reflective of the whole truth about society and, thus, more serious. Alex Kruse was always serious about his art. He learned from his Ash Can teachers that by seeking out the ironic, sad, humorous, and ordinary, one found a much greater diversity of subject and mood than did the impressionists, who sought mostly the bucolic, the gentler and optimistic holiday mood. For Kruse, life in New York was frequently not attractive and it was all too often cruel and ironic. He learned, however, that his art should reflect the environment he observed. As he gained in his skill to depict this true side of New York-based genre, he was praised openly for his images (both prints and paintings) and he grew in his aesthetic, finding inner reward as well.

Actually, it took several decades for the art world to eliminate representational art from its contemporary exhibition spaces, but, for virtually all but a few artists, there was little market and even less press for their pictures. Thus, for a man like Alex Kruse who was born in 1888 and made art under the tutelage of some of America's masters of twentieth century realism, why shouldn't he join the ranks of abstractionists just to get into exhibitions, just to get reviews, just to be fashionable, just to sell— why shouldn't he—just to live? But with the same tenacity that he braved the cultural elements to reach artistic maturity, he also clung to the general principles of the Ash Can mode so that he could refine his imagery. This he thought might take a lifetime, regardless of what changes took place in the art world he knew so well.

There are instances in the history of art in which the art tells us very little about the life of an artist and his aesthetic motivations. In reading these pages and learning more about Alex Kruse, the focus of his own imagery becomes clear and one is also provided some insight into his art criticism. No doubt others will write even more about this artist-critic, who was almost as appreciative of others' art as he was of his own. In that regard, he was unselfish and strove to find qualities in art of all types that other, less sophisticated eyes might miss. Certainly, his consummate art background was an asset for analysis and discussions in lectures and art columns. He considered it a privilege to rub shoulders with some of America's great makers and shakers who gave him a head start, but aesthetic intuition the likes of Alex Kruse could never be generated vicariously. He took his cultural responsibilities very seriously. Though he might occasionally reveal his cynicism or create satire to prove a point, in so doing he stripped away the superfluous to get at the real, just as he did in his own art. Some critic constituents saw him as one either courageous or foolhardy for exhibiting his own work while yet writing weekly art reviews. As a full-time wearer of both hats, he knew that his artist-critic role put him in harm's way, but he was willing to risk his reputation to give all he had to art. Quoted from one of his 1935 "Art to Heart Talks" columns, Kruse's own words best summarize his motivation: "He who never does anything never makes any mistakes. The reason why so many of the cuttingly critical in print never produce any bad paintings is due to the fact that they never paint. The enlightened art critic of today, with his highly developed sensitiveness, has grasped the full significance of the art of criticism. Therefore, he looks more for the silver lining inside of the clouds-upon-clouds of art production, until he finds virtues that over-shadow the many faults of many artists."

Perhaps one of the most important aspects of this text is that it tells not of the typical American rags to riches story, but proves the value of perseverance in art. Quite unlike George Bellows, who was transplanted from the Midwest to New York and burst upon the scene with youthful enthusiasm, Kruse grew up in the very environment that midwestern artists interpreted as the new essence of American art. Just as Bellows assimilated Henri's realist manifesto to synaesthetically depict the sights and sounds of New York with unparalleled machismo style, Kruse extracted some of the same subjects. At first glance, the differences in their pictures are monumental; moreover, there is no mutuality between these disparate personalities. Yet, despite the obvious differences in social and cultural backgrounds, both artists were similarly motivated. Their driving mutual interest was to understand and apply Henri's mode of realism. Another mutual motivation was their interest in the American socialist movement, *The Masses,* and other liberal ideals which could be exploited in the art. But the real sameness of their lives and art was their devotion to forthrightness in art, unbridled honesty in presenting New York City as it really existed. The difference was that Bellows had to learn how to see it while Kruse knew no other scenery—Kruse was streetwise in the first part of this century and he understood urban life as few outsiders could. In fact, this is the point of departure for Kruse from his constituency. Notwithstanding the fact that he was never an official member of the slightly older group of Henri-Sloan rebels, his association with Luks, Jerome Myers, and others provided the kind of inspiration which helped him to see the dowdy urban environment as a treasure trove of the best subject matter America had to offer.

As we study his art, however, we see that Kruse's view was somewhat different from his mentors—his images could never be seen as the product of an outsider looking in; instead, they are discovered and created from the perspective of an insider, one who knew the secrets about New

Yorkers that only a native could know. So, Kruse's candid glimpses are always insightful depictions of urban life, honest, sometimes humorous portrayals of common people caught in the fray of the city.

There is no doubt that Kruse saw his subjects as real-life actors on the urban proscenium, but he always observed them from backstage. Like them, he was truly one of the actors and never one of the audience who observed at a distance. Perhaps it was because he knew so much about the city, its urbanity, its inwards and its facades, that in spite of his assimilation of the Ash Can tradition, his images were nonetheless significantly distinct. Perhaps it was because New York was no surprise to Kruse—the all-too-often shocking views of deprivation and cultural contrasts were not jarring revelations to him. Therefore, with the exception of a few large "world view" subjects, Kruse's images are never sensational or melodramatic, but always intuitively subtle, frequently focusing on the jocoseness of the genre he captures from city dwellers. Even when he was in the midst of New York's theater culture, the imagery he chose there was not stereotypically dramatic, but perspicacious, witty, and sometimes approaching surrealism.

For all of the obvious humanism in Kruse's approach to the urban subjects he loved, there was also the reflectively spiritual side of his art. His optimistic attitude about life in general, in spite of its ironies, and his unswerving belief in mankind, resulted in an art which was forthright.

Kruse understood the principles of art so well, he could easily have converted to abstraction. Actually, the maturation of his art paralleled that of abstraction in America. But Kruse knew that to understand does not guarantee conversion. Kruse was an exceedingly liberal thinker. Once again from the column "Art to Heart Talks," his own words prove his appreciative tolerance of the movement that would all but snuff out his own art mode, but his belief in the endurance of aesthetics was greater than his own ego: "There are those who know how to draw, and those who know how to see; those who feel interpretively, and those who depend entirely upon their physical eyes and free-hand draftsmanship." He continued: "The underlying success of the great modern masters of mental, emotional, and technical innovation is an open secret. They are at heart the eternal students, never ceasing to experiment."

Even when Kruse departed New York City and found new subjects in different environments to draw and paint, he was motivated by the same inner aesthetic demand, that is, to extract only that momentary slice of life which revealed something special about human behavior. Certainly, he was not the only artist to do so, but the results are fascinating, even compelling, studies and finished statements that reveal a unique ability to see beyond the mundane.

Although he appreciated America's European art heritage, he thought there was something amazingly rich and diversified about his fellow citizens, regardless of race or religion. Kruse was a fiercely loyal American and believed that the Constitution gave him the right to be critical when he thought it necessary. He was an American in the ideal sense of the word: he believed that all Americans should have the right to pursue that which was best for them. For him, it was observing the realities of that pursuit and recording it for ages to come that was the driving force of his life. Art was life for Alexander Kruse, as one will learn from the following pages.

Richard H. Love
Chicago, August, 1994

Early drawing. Untitled.

Acknowledgments

This book and the "rediscovery" activities it commemorates results from the great sensitivity and tremendous depth of knowledge displayed by Richard H. Love, whom I first encountered in 1975. My mother had died months earlier and I suddenly found myself with full responsibility for the handling, treatment, and accorded respect that I felt the body of work left by my father deserved. I brought several dozen slides to Richard Love, who responded both positively and wisely.

Shortly thereafter, Richard and Gerry Love visited our home in Tujunga, CA, and immersed themselves in the collected works, papers, and assorted memorabilia that made up the A. Z. Kruse Collection. Arrangements were made to ship all the paintings, books, drawings, and assorted papers to Chicago, where Richard Love supervised the process of having them recorded as part of the National Archives of Art.

Part of Richard Love's great understanding of American art was that the type of work my father had produced—social realism or creative realism (also called the Ash Can School)—had been shunted aside in the orgy of nonrepresentation that dominated the scene for several decades.

Richard Love has displayed patience to match his great foresight. He provided continuous storage, insurance, and loving care for the works of A. Z. Kruse through the long years until he felt the time was right for the major re-emergence commemorated by this book.

Encountering the honesty and integrity, to say nothing of the growing love, that has matured between Richard and Gerry Love and Ben and Betti Kruse since 1975 adds up to an unparalleled stroke of good fortune in my own fifty-plus years of working and business experience. Relationships with this level of warmth are a true blessing that deserve unqualified acknowledgment and thanks.

Through the years, the hands-on care for the A. Z. Kruse Collection has fallen to Bruce Bachman, who plays so many critical roles in the ongoing operation of the Love Galleries. This book could not have been put together in its final form without Bruce's professional, highly competent assistance.

Julie Love Hosier, as she has assumed responsibilities in the management of Love Galleries, has contributed to maintenance of the enthusiasm that has represented essential support for the unveiling of A. Z. Kruse's works before the public.

Vytus Babusis of the Love Galleries greatly eased the work of writing and assembling this book through his tireless services in assembling, organizing, and summarizing the vast number of documents left by Alex Kruse.

I also wish to thank the rest of the Love Galleries staff—Thomas J. Hosier, Roy R. Younger, Evelyn J. Kemp, Camilla L. Hurych, Robert D. Freelon, and Lacey Freelon—for their always-ready help during research sessions in Chicago and during setup and implementation of plans for the Kruse exhibition.

Immediate credit for development of this book itself belongs to Sally Davis, editor-in-chief of Northwest Publishing Inc., Salt Lake City. Our relationship with Sally began with the excellent job she did as editor of the autobiographical novel based on the experiences of Alex Kruse, *East of Broadway*. This biography began with discussions about the best way to develop a suitable catalog for the A. Z. Kruse rediscovery exhibition scheduled by the Love Galleries for September, 1994. Sally laid down the challenge which led to complete pre-press development of this work in less than ninety days. Sally's encouragement and support, in turn, would have been impossible without the understanding and complete backing of James Van Treese, president, and Jim Perkins, general manager, of Northwest Publishing.

In recent years, Bettijune and I have been honored with the extension of privileges as reader-scholars at the Henry E. Huntington Library and Art Gallery, located near our home in Pasadena. The extensive collection of art reference materials in the Library provided an invaluable resource for initial research about the period and the people with whom Alex Kruse lived, learned, and worked. In particular, Amy Meyers, Curator of American Art, and Diedre Cantrell, department secretary, both of whom are connected with the Huntington's Virginia Steele Scott Collection, extended cooperation in providing photographs of works by John Sloan and George Luks for inclusion in this book.

The Pasadena Public Library, which boasts an excellent collection of art publications, made it possible for us to borrow and use at home a number of books that helped provide historic background during preparation of the manuscript for this book.

Finally, for the privilege of knowing you so intimately and for the honor of being your son, thanks Dad.

Benedict Kruse
Pasadena, CA   August, 1994

Early drawing. Untitled.

1
Starting Out

Alexander Zerdin Kruse entered life on February 9, 1888, at the time oblivious to a catastrophe that engulfed his parents and millions of other adult New Yorkers. The setting was a tiny tenement flat on Allen Street, a northern boundary of the area generally identified as the Lower East Side, the teaming ghetto at the southern tip of Manhattan peopled by primarily in-migrating eastern and southern Europeans arriving by the hundreds of thousands in any given year.

The event was the Blizzard of Eighty-Eight, which retained its distinction as the most crippling natural disaster to strike New York City until a larger blizzard crippled a larger, more mechanized city in December, 1947. From there, Alex Kruse would recite in later years when relatives recounted the event, it seemed safe to predict that things had to get better.

[A birth certificate found in the Kruse family effects lists Alexander's birthday as February 29, 1888. However, he celebrated his birthday on February 9 throughout his life. Other documents, such as school records and teaching licenses, confirm this earlier date. He used to joke about this discrepancy, saying that he changed his birthday because he didn't want to be limited to celebrating only once every four years. A more plausible explanation: given the Blizzard and other preoccupations, his parents didn't get around to registering the birth until February 29.]

Alex Kruse was reminded about the circumstances of his birth much later when, on his eighty-third birthday, he survived a devastating Los Angeles earthquake in the same manner as the blizzard that coincided with his birth—he slept through the whole thing.

In between, Kruse witnessed vitally important developments unparalleled in the history of humanity. A boy whose main source of transportation was horse-drawn street cars lived to clock in tens of thousands of miles behind the wheel of an automobile and went on to experience a number of white-knuckle flights on jet aircraft that carried him between his beloved New York and his final home in Los Angeles.

Less noticed, but just as significant for an artist with his sensitivity, was a cultural evolution that saw Alex Kruse's New York become a world-class center of the arts: fine arts, literature, and performing arts. The times were right for this massive cultural transformation. The United States was well into a larger transition that followed the comparatively late arrival of the Industrial Revolution, the major technological explosion that had transformed England and parts of Europe decades earlier. America was in transition from a bygone status as a nation of embattled farmers into a world-leading industrial and financial colossus whose guiding entrepreneurs were ready to support a move toward cultural and artistic leadership. Alex Kruse was born in the right place and at the right time to observe these massive changes, then to carry forward a trend that pioneered new dimensions in American art, a movement that helped to make New York a focal point in the art world at large.

Social historians, who have offered voluminous comments on the conditions that prevailed in the lower reaches of Manhattan Island during the final decades of the nineteenth century, evoke images of massive poverty amid dirty, unhealthful living conditions. Unquestionably, the Lower East Side was a shamefully neglected, exploited slum area. Unquestionably also, the Kruses were poor. But there was also a smattering of richness that touched their lives.

Sigmund Krushinsky, Alex's father, grew up in Silesia, a slice of Europe that was sometimes part of Poland; at other times, Germany. Still in his teens, he migrated to Berlin, where he became a graduate student and scholar fascinated by the socialist writings that were pouring forth in the German language he adored throughout his life. He was enthralled by the principles expounded by Marx, Engels, Goethe, Kant, and others. But in 1880, disillusioned and embittered by mounting anti-semitism on one side and, on the other, the haughty insults of German Jews who referred to him as a "verdammte Polock," he emigrated to the United States, where his name was shortened during immigration processing, as happened to millions of other new Americans.

New York in 1880 had little use for erudition from its immigrants. Even Sigmund Kruse's high level of literacy and his linguistic skills—he was conversant in seven languages—didn't matter. What was needed was hard work, of which there was no shortage. The closest Sigmund Kruse could come to the intellectual existence to which he aspired was as a cigar maker in a factory situated in a basement on the Bowery. As a cigar maker, Sigmund lucked into a hospitable set of surroundings for a person who was by then a committed socialist and intellectual idealist.

Sigmund Kruse, c. 1870.

Cigar makers were the intelligentsia among blue collar immigrant workers. The intellectually active and curious were attracted by the nature of the job. Cigar makers operated in teams of four who worked around a single table with positions allocated for different tasks. The work was laid out so that only three of the "bench brothers" were busy at any given moment. The idle brother helped the others overcome the boredom of their repetitive tasks by serving as the "reader." His interim job was to read to his fellow workers, keeping them alert and interested as their hands labored at their mindless pursuits. At Sigmund Kruse's bench, philosophy and socialism were in. The brothers took turns reading from works of the likes of Kant, Schopenhauer, Goethe, and, of course, Marx and Engels.

They also dreamed. One brother, a rare Englishman in that German-speaking enclave, dreamt about labor organizations that would enhance the lives of workers. Since most cigar makers spoke German as their first language, language was a potential obstacle to organizing the cigar workers as America's first craft union. So, as they worked, Sigmund and the others taught their brother, Samuel Gompers, to speak German. The basic concepts that evolved into the American Federation of Labor were, in effect, born and nurtured at that cigar-making bench in a Bowery basement. Sigmund Kruse was a charter member of both the cigar-makers union and the AFL.

Another brother, who had been a promising music student in Germany, went on to become a major musical and theatrical producer. When Alex Kruse was seventeen, one of his early jobs as an artist was painting scenery for this former bench brother, Oscar Hammerstein, Sr., who founded a musical theater and then went on to build the Manhattan Opera Company, which competed for a time with the Metropolitan Opera.

Sigmund's idealism and socialism, however, were relegated to a status of avocation. In Germany, he had been considered as a budding writer. Alex's papers also reported that his father harbored an interest in sculpture. In the United States, he was so poorly paid in one effort at writing a newspaper article that he gave up on any thoughts of cultural pursuits as a livelihood—and also tried mightily to discourage the impractical dreams about art in his son.

Sigmund pressed Alex to go to work at the earliest feasible age; the father was obsessed with the need to bring money into the house. Even though his earnings were at the top of the blue-collar scale, the family took in a boarder in the already-crowded flat at 133 Henry Street to which they had moved shortly after Alex's birth. The boarder's rent helped cover the added expense of rent in a building with inside plumbing—a combination bathtub and sink in the kitchen and one toilet, invariably called a "water closet," situated in the hallway and shared by four families.

Lena Zerdin Kruse, c. 1870.

Lena Zerdin Kruse, emigrated from St. Petersburg, Russia, along with one sister, Rachel. Born in 1862, she was two years younger than Sigmund, whom she met in New York. An old family story demonstrates Lena's gentle humor—as well as her belief in predestination. As it happened, Sigmund's proposal of marriage came just a few days after Steve Brodie's reported daredevil leap off the Brooklyn Bridge in July, 1886. The newspapers were full of accounts which credited Brodie with being the first person to survive a jump from the bridge that had been constructed just three years earlier. "Well," Lena was said to have responded, "Steve Brodie took a chance." They were married a few months later.

Never a strong woman, Lena Zerdin Kruse became chronically frail and continually ill following childbirth. She was under doctors' care during most of Alex's youth, always doing her best to care for her son and, above all, to let him know he was loved. This condition helped lead to a closeness between the mother and her attentive son. Lena had no more children. But she outlived a number of doctors and their frequent pronouncements that she had a short time to live. Lena Kruse developed an unwavering faith in a healing God to whose oversight she attributed a lifespan that extended for seventy-six years.

His mother's Bible and his father's socialism, for all their contradictory inferences, contributed notably to Alex Kruse's artistic temperament and vision. Both influences helped him to visualize and empathize with the plight of the poor, struggling, plodding immigrants and their preoccupation with survival. Survival had its inevitable rough spots. The Lower East

Side was a tough, crime-ridden neighborhood, one that could leave scars on even the most innocent residents. Throughout his adult life, for example, Alex Kruse experienced nightmares stemming from the childhood experience of waking to find a burglar crawling through the window of the family bedroom from the fire escape that faced onto Henry Street. As he recounted the incident in later years, his screams drove the burglar off. But the vision never left him; he would see the same intruder and wake up with the same screams in nightmares that followed him into his final years.

My Aunt, Rachel Medalie.

In Alexander Kruse's Lower East Side, the impact of permeating poverty was cushioned in important ways by the extended family of which he was a closeknit part. Lena Kruse was close to her sister, Rachel Zerdin Medalie, who lived in an adjoining flat of the tenement at 133 Henry Street. The Medalie family included four cousins, a boy and three girls, who were a constant source of youthful companionship and encouragement and who maintained a lifelong relationship with Alex and his family.

On the other side of the family and across Henry Street in a similar tenement lived Sigmund's younger sister, Gusie Greenberg. She raised three sons who were younger than Alex. Although day-to-day closeness between Alex and his Greenberg cousins was not the same as with the Medalie clan, a sense of family loyalty remained and has endured into the next generation.

The world that encompassed and played an important role in shaping Alex Kruse was geographically small, bounded by Canal Street on the North, Broadway on the West, the Battery on the South, and the East River. Within the confines of this tight geographic world, immigrant parents did what was necessary to adjust and survive as they became aware that the American Dream was a hoax and that there was no turning back over the vast ocean which now separated them from the assorted hatreds and privations they had left in Europe. From ghettos scattered through Eastern Europe they had come. In a new and only slightly different ghetto they continued to find themselves.

While parents struggled, the children of the large immigrant families amused themselves on the dirty, inhospitable streets that were too hot in summer and much too cold in winter. This was an era that prized children for the work they could do and money they could bring into the home at early ages. The means of survival were close at hand. Most of the necessities of everyday life could be procured from pushcarts that lined most streets and crowded especially into the open area in and around nearby Grand Street. The English-basements of most tenements also contained a variety of shops overseen by families who waited on trade in the rooms facing the street and who lived behind their stores.

For tens of thousands of huddled immigrants, the Lower East Side was the main reality of life that existed pretty much as a world within itself, including schools to which Alex and his peers were dispatched with great expectations and close scrutiny of report cards, a Yiddish theater featuring everything from Shakespeare to a continual procession of melodramas and musical comedies, and, of particular importance to Alex and a select group of close-knit friends, an active settlement house, the Eastside Educational Alliance. The Educational Alliance was at once a training ground and a kind of finishing school that prepared East Siders for survival in the greater, grander world that lay north of Canal Street.

During toddler and pre-school stages of development, the younger children were looked after by their older siblings or cousins. The streets served as their playgrounds and provided their pre-school educational experiences. Life was grubby and grimy. But it also contained large measures of love, concern for the present, and unbounded aspirations for the future of the new generation—a vision that became the real American Dream for the denizens of the ghetto. Today was about survival; tomorrow was oriented toward hope.

The ghetto children created their own games and fun times, some of which are described by an older Alex Kruse in his diaries:

> These unforgettable reflections sometimes appear in the semblance of a cinematized celluloid reel. At other times, this sort of memory lane review seems to take on the form of animated pictographs. Episodes of those childhood days pertain to events that had taken place among playmates between ages of about four to six.
>
> Two of the older children were ring-leaders in such games as "Follow Master," Hide & Seek, Cops and Robbers. But a game of lasting memory for me was the one they called "play acting."
>
> The ring leader of this game was the son of parents who were actors in the Yiddish theater. He was of primary school age. Therefore, we had late afternoon rehearsals.
>
> Then came the Saturday morning try-out without rehearsals. Just the leader's bossy directions. First of all, the out-houses [in the backyard] were used as reserved seats, with the doors flung widely open.
>
> That make-believe stage was the area between the out-houses and a large wooden water pump in the center of the yard. The youngsters sat around on the concrete stone floor between...
> In retrospect, it is easy to see the influence upon children of the then prevalent Nickelodeon Silent Moving Picture Houses.
>
> That [end of play] was followed by HooRays and Bravos with wild applause, while a linen bed-spread was being used as a stage curtain and was being pulled across the overhead washlines, behind the big

wooden water pump.

Adding to the mixed noises already permeating the air was that home-spun trio striking up that then-popular tune "Sweet Rosy O'Grady." That trio consisted of a harmonica player, a girl humming through a comb covered with a sheet of toilet tissue, and the drummer boy who manipulated his drum-sticks vigorously on a metal milk-can cover which he balanced between his knees.

After viewing a movie in 1967 on avant garde sculptural escapades, or, as he said "junk yard sculpture," Alexander Kruse recalled another youthful game:

>...between the ages of 10 and 12, it was always in some kid's back yard on Henry Street between Rutgers and Pike Streets, where we'd stuff a pair of pants and a shirt with newspapers and rags and even excelsior when we found it. Joe Cooper, who was choir boy in the synagogue where his father was cantor in the Pike Street shool [synagogue], lent a helping hand. The younger boys like Eddie Cantor or Willie Howard would bring in some masks—we called them forefaces (they were made of papier-mache and cost a cent apiece) and put them over an egg-shaped head constructed of newspapers and kept together with some cord or twine—and they would impersonate ventriloquists.
>
>One would shake the head up and down or to the right and left—depending upon the questions and answers while the other talked out of the side of his mouth with his head turned aside to hide his lip movements.
>
>Once they put one of those stuffed figures in a woman's clothes and big picture hat and set it up on a neighbor's bicycle—
>
>The owner of the bicycle was a street cleaner (he had a steady job). He was so delighted, he treated the kids, the whole eight of them, to Hokey Poky ice-cream bars. He left it...[in] the yard for days and brought friends and neighbors to enjoy the fun.

Though poverty was a common denominator, diversity was a fact of life. People followed the habits and spoke the languages they brought with them. Children with good memories and a will to please their elders needed multiple languages to interact with parents, extended families, and neighbors. Alex Kruse spoke three languages during his early years and acquired a fourth as he prepared for a traditional Bar Mitzvah at thirteen.

English was primary, recognized universally in the ghetto as the language of opportunity for children. German in the Kruse household was the literary language that showed the educational status of the family. Both Sigmund and Lena were literate in German, the language of the newspapers, journals, and books that they read profusely. Yiddish was the universal language of East European Jews, the mother tongue of their tribulations and survival through centuries of abuse. The Kruses and everyone else they related to were fluent in Yiddish. New York supported two daily newspapers published in the Yiddish language, as well as a number of Yiddish theaters. In effect, Yiddish was the jargon of the streets of the Lower East Side. From the time he was a small boy, Alex Kruse spoke these three languages—English, German, and Yiddish—interchangeably.

Hebrew was the language of prayer. Like most Jewish boys at that time and place, Alex Kruse attended Hebrew school after his days in P.S. 2 on Henry Street. Hebrew lessons commenced at age nine and continued until his Bar Mitzvah at thirteen. Hebrew then got regular use as Alex accompanied Sigmund to their synagogue on Friday evenings and Saturday mornings for some time after his Bar Mitzvah. Years later, notes he wrote to his wife, Anna, were often signed in Hebrew.

As a mark of pride, Alex Kruse, with his parents' encouragement, wrote and delivered his Bar Mitzvah speech in highly literate, carefully enunciated German. He memorized the speech before he delivered it. Early in life, this was just one of several demonstrations of his elephant-like memory. Years later, when he was seventy-six prior to attending the Bar Mitzvah of his grandson, Martin, he repeated his own Bar Mitzvah speech verbatim, still enunciating in flawless German. That caliber of memory stood Alex Kruse in good stead as an artist. Up to his final days, he was able to recall and paint figures and landscapes flawlessly from his seemingly infinite memory capacity.

East Siders grew to maturity understanding hard work and ambition. Through the years, the young people who emigrated as children or who were born into immigrant families that poured through the New York gateway during the last decades of the nineteenth century contributed mightily to the prosperity and the economic and cultural evolution of the country as a whole and to the world at large. Alex's own contemporaries at P.S. 2 on Henry Street and after school sessions at the Alliance included the likes of Edward G. Robinson, Samuel Chotzinoff, Eddie Cantor, Irving Berlin, and his first cousin, George Zerdin Medalie, who became a pre-eminent corporate attorney, then Deputy Attorney General for the Southern District of New York, and later New York Supreme Court Justice in the Albany Appellate Division.

Alex, who kept track of the careers of his boyhood friends, later wrote:

> …Little did we even dream that ten or fifteen years later or maybe twenty that Joe Cooper would become a vaudeville headliner with the popular Empire City Quartet—or that Samy [sic] Chotzinoff would turn out to become piano accompanist [for] Ephrim Zimbalist and Jasha Heifitz and music critic of the N. Y. Post and finally Music

Director of the National Broadcasting Company Orchestra, [or that] Eddie Cantor and Willy Howard would become such outstanding stars in show business…

During his toddling and preschool years, the streets were the boundaries of Alex Kruse's activities and the focus of his interests. From the time he could hold a pencil, he drew pictures on whatever paper was available. When he was old enough to navigate the stairs of 133 Henry Street on his own, one of his regular chores was to take the newspapers down to the ground floor trash cans after his father finished reading them. Alex would rifle through the papers to find pages with limited printed content. He would cut these up and use them for crayon drawings which he generated in endless streams.

His subject matter came from his surroundings. Alex Kruse developed an early fascination with the street people who surrounded him. He would draw images of the peddlers he encountered, become fascinated with portraying an organ grinder and his monkey, be enraptured by street entertainers who abounded and continued to provide subject matter for the works he created throughout his youth and young-adult years. After he entered school, his notebooks became an amalgam of visual impressions and mandatory homework assignments. Young Alex earned more than his share of raps on the knuckles from rulers wielded by teachers who admonished him to do class lessons rather than drawings of fellow students.

The first overt encouragement for his artwork that Alex Kruse reported in later years came from a storefront artist who subsisted by doing cheap, quick pastel portraits or colored drawings from family tintypes. To help meet expenses, the artist sublet part of his store to a local bookie. Alex Kruse first encountered the artist when he walked with his father to deliver cigars that Sigmund sold to derive extra income for the family. The factory where Sigmund worked permitted workers to take home, for personal use, a quota of cigars without the brand-name bands. Frugal Sigmund made a deal to sell his personal supply to a tailor whose store was adjacent to the artist's. Young Alex watched so intently through the window as the artist worked that he was invited inside for some rudimentary lessons and encouragement. With pennies saved with the help and connivance of his mother, Alex was able to purchase a regular notepad, which he immediately put to use for intensive sketching in the neighborhood.

When Alex Kruse was ten or eleven and engrossed in drawing an organ grinder and monkey on busy Grand Street, a jovial gentleman with a big smile and a whiskey breath tapped him on the shoulder. The adult introduced himself as a colleague, a fellow artist. The stranger said his name was George Luks. Recently returned from an assignment as an

The Organ Grinder. (Oil, 18" x 14").

illustrator covering the Spanish-American War in Cuba, Luks was working as an illustrator and cartoonist on the *New York World* while also making a name for himself as a painter with a bright future.

Right then and there, the sidewalks of Grand Street became Alex's first impromptu art school as Luks made suggestions about composition and the use of lines and shadows in drawing. Luks borrowed the youngster's pad and pencil and demonstrated professional technique. Teaching through demonstration was George Luks's way, as Alex Kruse was to learn in his maturing years as an art student. Kruse himself adopted much the same methodology of instruction through demonstration when he himself became a successful teacher.

According to later stories, Luks gave the youngster some pocket change with a mandate to go buy some paints and brushes, then report to the Educational Alliance in the fall to sign up for a class being taught by Luks's friend, Henry McBride, already a well-known writer on the arts and a prominent "uptown" volunteer who ventured into the ghetto to bring culture to the unwashed masses.

Alex Kruse had company when he lined up to register at the Educational Alliance at the end of the first day of school in September, 1899. With him were two friends lining up for their first formal training as musicians. In later years, they fabricated—but agreed upon details of—a story about the beginnings of their cultural education. The friends were Samuel Chotzinoff, who later became the impresario who brought Arturo Toscanini to the United States as conductor of the NBC Symphony, and David Epstein, who became a successful violist and member of the NBC Symphony.

Their story: Davey Epstein and Sam Chotzinoff were on line ahead of

Alex Kruse, in that order. They all intended to sign up together in the Alliance orchestra. Davey Epstein got the last portable instrument, a violin. Sam Chotzinoff got the last seat in the orchestra—at the piano. Then somebody stuck a paintbrush into Alex Kruse's hand and they were all off toward their life's work.

In reality, it was a stick of charcoal that was first placed in Alex Kruse's hand by Henry McBride. McBride was already well known as a critic and columnist for a number of art magazines. He was also a recognized artist in his own right, as well as an "uptowner" with the kind of conscience that lured highly qualified people into volunteering for service in the Alliance and similar institutions. In the McBride class, Kruse and his fellow East Siders began with practical lessons in anatomy sketching. McBride used plaster molds from Greek and Roman statues, as well as "anatomy busts" with cutaway portions showing muscle and bone structures, as subjects from which his beginning students were required to sketch. Charcoal proved the ideal medium for learning to represent form and tone values.

These initial lessons stood Alex Kruse in good stead throughout his life. Later, he acquired anatomy busts of his own, which he referred to frequently to refresh his sense of the human form. The plaster casts remained in his possession until his death.

Later, as he progressed to more advanced classes at the Alliance, Alex Kruse had an opportunity to study with a man who was to become, like Luks and other contemporaries, a close friend. He was Jerome Myers, a pioneer in presenting New York street scenes and street people as fit subjects for artistic rendition. Myers also gave young Alex Kruse his first training in portrait painting.

During his years at the Alliance, Alex Kruse gained a broad exposure and built serious skills that covered a broad range of media. Following initial training in charcoal sketching, he learned to put the litho crayon to effective use, then went on to work in oils, and to make his first forays into printmaking. The first known etching produced by Alex Kruse was created when he was thirteen, in 1901. This proved to be the skill base for a career which led to his recognition, during the 1930s, as one of America's preeminent printmakers.

It can be difficult to imagine the caliber of work done and the intensity of the students who appeared at these after-school and Sunday workshops in one of the poorest, most downtrodden neighborhoods in the entire country. This seemingly unlikely environment provided a breeding ground for talents such as Jo Davidson, Jacob Epstein, Abraham Walkowitz, and a number of others who went on to gain national and international reputations.

Yet these budding young artists held on to the friends of their neighborhood, trying to be part of both worlds, as Alex wrote in his later years:

After school hours, most of the boys played crap (dice) for buttons, and some used playing cards in such games as 21, poker, and casino. Cigarette box tops were often used for betting. Those of us young art students on my block kept our art study a secret from our buddies because drawing and painting was associated with being a sissy. Nevertheless we'd become one of the boys when playtime was in order for us art minded kids. That included at least one afternoon session in the outdoor Seward Park gym.

The Alliance experience had a lifelong impact on Alex Kruse, as reflected in the following excerpt from a notebook entry in 1969:

Actually, it was Henry McBride who, before he became the generally acknowledged dean of American art critics, came to the Lower East Side as a teacher from the Trenton School of Industrial Design to organize art classes at the Educational Alliance. These classes were for school children two afternoons a week and for adults three evenings a week. Having been a painting buddy of Jerome Myers in Paris and having realized the high creative standard of Jerome Myers art, he naturally assigned Myers to take charge of the Sunday painting classes.

At this point, I must digress long enough to say that sincerity and integrity were important character gifts that both Henry McBride and Jerome Myers both possessed. It became obvious even to me as a teenager that McBride, after the studio building in Paris burned down, together with all his work painted up to that period, became discouraged enough to turn to teaching and writing so that he could at least be helpful to fellow artists and keep his head in the art atmosphere even though he could never stir up enough courage to keep on painting after that fire, a consuming catastrophe which swallowed the works produced during the best years of his life. It punctured his ambition ever to try again to be a painter. Nevertheless, there are a few scanty drawings which a good friend owns which indicate that art didn't give up Henry McBride altogether.

Alex Kruse continued his studies at the Alliance until he graduated from eighth grade at P.S. 2, the elementary school across the street on Henry Street. After that, as was common in virtually all the neighborhood families, he was expected to go to work. The paying jobs he found and held covered his own expenses and enabled him to contribute to expenses in maintaining his parents' home. For many years, he worked at a range of different occupations, often holding down more than one job at a time. These jobs were stopgaps required while he poured his soul and all the spare time he could muster into building skills and talents as an artist. For two years following graduation from P.S. 2, Kruse worked full time as an office boy and also filled virtually all free time left to him with pursuits of art study and continuing education. The following are some descriptions of his work experiences between ages fourteen and sixteen taken from diaries:

My first distaste for a business career started when I was an office boy working for a hosiery and underwear commission house between the ages of fourteen and sixteen…working from eight a.m. to 6 p.m. six days a week…Among other chores, I was in charge of what was then known as the Letter Copying press. Letter size cloths were dampened and a tissue page was placed over it and the letter to be copied over that and waterproof cardboard over that. Then the book of tissues was closed and put into the letter press topped by an iron disc. Then it was tightened by winding the wheel down as tight as the iron cover clamp would allow. I was in charge of this book of tissue letter copies. One day the boss came into the office with a hosiery manufacturer. This hefty, prosperous looking six-footer heard the boss order me to find a letter canceling the order on the hosiery company this man represented. I found it. The man told the boss he was satisfied and apologized. I could have played the boss a dirty trick because I remembered that the boss tore that letter up after I copied it.

I made it a point to find time to attend Henry McBride's life class two evenings a week…and attended the Sunday morning painting class during these two years…But most exciting culturally I found in attendance at the Thomas Davidson School [a branch of the Educational Alliance] three evenings a week. It qualified us youngsters to acquire our high-school equivalence credits…Saturday evenings I taught a children's art class in the Thomas Davidson School.

As another of his occupations, he sold shoes, mostly on a part-time basis for the chain that eventually was absorbed into the Kinney organization, still a major shoe retailer. Later, he also operated his own shoe store in Harlem for a number of years.

In approximately 1905, he received some of his first paying assignments as an artist from his father's old friend, Oscar Hammerstein, Sr. By then, Hammerstein had left cigar making and opened a busy, successful musical theater uptown on Twenty-third Street. Alex Kruse worked there as a scene painter. When he wasn't actively working, he would hang around producing drawings that remained in his possession as working resources throughout his life and also served as guides for a number of later prints and paintings. Many performers who later became major theatrical personalities gained their early experience at Hammerstein's theater. Among the drawings still in the family is one of Ted Lewis on stage at the Hammerstein theater. Another development related to the Hammerstein connection accrued to Alex Kruse's close friend, Samuel Chotzinoff, who came to the attention of the music world when he was hired to play piano behind a curtain in a play that called for the leading man to be a music teacher. The actor learned enough motions to convince audiences; Chotzinoff provided the actual music.

Kruse worked at a number of commercial art studios doing advertising illustrations. His specialty as a commercial illustrator was drawing hands and feet for fashion advertisements. His qualifications in advertising illustration during those days prior to general use of photoengraving enabled him, some two decades later, to make a transition as an art director for a major photoengraving company, a connection that put him into contact with many leading retailers and publishing houses.

While he was still in his teens, Alex Kruse started a teaching career that evolved into a lifelong activity. He secured part-time positions as an art instructor, first at the Thomas Davidson School and then, later, at Christie House (a settlement house), and the Young Men's Hebrew Association.

While working and studying art, Kruse, as noted above, also enhanced his academic education through classes at the Thomas Davidson School, where he gained the equivalent of a high school diploma, and the Rand School, a socialist institution. At both these schools he also took classes in art as well as in academic subjects.

In 1904, a major tragedy impacted Kruse personally and emotionally. The resulting trauma affected his sense of values and social outlook for many years. At sixteen, Alex Kruse was in love with a girl next door, Jennie, a younger sister of his close friend, David Epstein, the musician. The couple considered themselves committed to each other and planned to marry eventually.

The young lady, fifteen and hard at work as a seamstress in a clothing factory, was invited by her forelady to a day's outing and picnic sponsored by the local Lutheran Church to which the supervisor belonged. The festive day, planned as a treat and an escape opportunity for women and children only, was to include an excursion-boat ride up the East River to a campground where a picnic and games were to be held.

The trip started early on the morning of June 15, 1904, when the excursion steamer, the *General Slocum,* pulled away from a lower Manhattan dock with some 1,100-plus wives, young women, and children aboard, while hordes of husbands, sweethearts, and fathers bid farewell. As the *Slocum* pulled away from the dock, a boiler exploded and the ship burst into flames. The ship's captain panicked, opting for a course of action that cost hundreds of lives. Instead of pulling back into the dock while there was still time for passengers to disembark on an orderly basis, he guided the ship into the East River and headed upstream toward North Brother's Island. By the time the ship made landfall, its structure was demolished and almost 900 passengers and crew members were dead, Alex's love among them.

The captain was convicted of manslaughter less than two weeks later, on June 28, 1904. But the trauma of the incident didn't subside with the trial. Nineteen years passed before Alex Kruse was ready to make a marriage commitment.

Long Island Peasant. (Oil, 12" x 16").

Astoria, L.I.
(Oil, 16" x 20").

City Hall Park. (Oil, 16" x 20").

Chewing Gum Vendor. (Oil, 16 1/4" x 24 1/4").

Friendly Card Game.
(Oil, 12" x 16").

Music Hall, Ted Lewis.
(Oil, 20" x 16").

A Boston Sunset.
(Tempera, 32 1/2" x 44 1/2").

Two Generations.
(Tempera, 32 1/2" x 44 1/2").

Portrait of Anna. (Oil, 24 1/4" x 20").

Liane.
(Oil, 12 1/4" x 14 1/2").

Luna Park Carousel. (Oil).

Cropsey Bridge, Coney Island.
(Oil, 24 1/4" x 20").

Outskirts of Coney Island.
(Oil, 12"x16").

Hauser's Hotel, Fire Island. (Oil, 16" x 20").

Studio Interior, Fire Island. (Oil, 16" x 20").

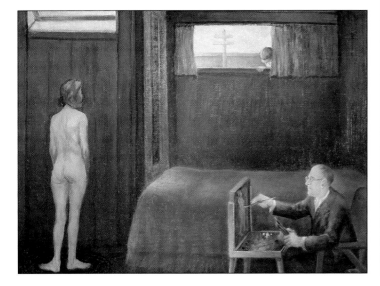

Observing Puppy, Fire Island. (Oil, 15 3/4" x 11 3/4").

Country Kitchen, Tessie.
(Oil, 17" x 16").

Below:
Pencil sketch with
color annotations for painting.

Country Wedding.
(Oil, 20" x 24").

2
Toward A Career in Art

In the fall of 1904, at sixteen, Alex Kruse was accepted as a scholarship student at the National Academy of Design. The entrance examination proved a breeze following his Educational Alliance training; he was required to submit a drawing of a full-length torso of a Greek sculpture. He attended classes days and covered expenses, including contributions to his parents' household, by selling shoes evenings and weekends.

Among his instructors at the Academy was Emil Carlsen. The curriculum at the Academy provided some important growth opportunities even though Kruse bridled under the inflexibility and lack of creative opportunity of the Academy's instructional methods. Much of the assigned work involved literal copying from traditional, classic, comparatively colorless and unimaginative paintings. Student renderings had to replicate the originals exactly. In later years, Alex would describe, mockingly, how one of the instructors used a surveyor's plumb line to check vertical alignment of elements of student canvases.

He described the experience as follows in one of his later diaries:

…When I was admitted as a student at the National Academy of Design after one week's examination drawing from a life-sized sculptured figure, I was astonished that the instructor advised us to get plumb lines to make sure we got the placement of the ankle of the foot of the model in line with the pit of the neck…I'd use that method only in the instructor's presence. But I felt that since it was a matter of becoming a better draughtsman, I mustn't antagonize the teacher.

The portrait painting instructor had the nasty habit of dipping a brush into white paint and slam bang some drastic correction lines of construction. That had its virtues only after his blotches of white paint was [sic] removed by my palette knife. It was a limited academic way for correcting the good-eye type of model-copying. This I kept up until I was able to paint and draw once again as I felt about what I saw. That's what Henry McBride kept drumming into our heads. So did Jerome Myers, who taught our juvenile Sunday morning painting class.

Nonetheless, the National Academy benefitted still-formative Alex Kruse in several important ways:

Kruse gained valuable opportunities to build skills in the basic craft of visual composition. The too-rigid discipline (at least for him) demanded at the Academy, which he resented and resisted, nonetheless taught him some lessons about creative composition and rearrangement of visual elements as they are found in nature, capabilities and resources that were put to good use in later years. The following are some benefits of the Academy experience described in one of Alex's diaries:

The year Emil Carlsen taught the morning still-life painting class, 1904, I found exciting because he gave class demonstrations of his method.

He was very conscious of surface textural variety. The first surprise among us curiosity [sic] youngsters was his breaking up an egg and separating the yoke from the white, which he spilled into a cup. He then added an equal amount of water and stirred it thoroughly with a brush handle. This he used as an underpainting medium with a simple palette of casein colors. Then he proceeded to paint the set up arrangement of a samovar with a few onions scattered in the foreground.

While painting, he frequently looked around at his encircled group of art students. He'd say "I hope you're following me closely. I can hear one of you asking why pick on onions and a Samovar. I'll tell you why. If you can get the color gradations [of] that wall behind the samovar and get the related color values of that samovar as a whole as related to the background, then you will find it much easier to get the three-dimensional form values in figure painting of men and women in their clothes or in the nude.

"Of course in the nude, there are bones and muscles to be considered. A separate study of that should not be neglected just as the anatomy of trees and variations of clouds should be studied before your attempts at landscape painting."

Mr. Carlsen painted the background first. Then he gave a masterly rendering of the brassy samovar. At intervals, he kept adding to the foreground in spots of color values related to the background and samovar. This he did intermittently with the onions, including color notations of the samovar.

One [student] did ask why he laid out the color spots of the objects before he started painting.

"I should have explained that in the beginning," he said. "At the outset of any painting, I do that for the same reason that an organist pulls out all the stops of the various instruments to be included in the piece he's about to play."

He continued painting while he talked and talked while he painted until he said: "Now the canvas is ready for framing. In conclusion I would like to say that when I find local color of an object becoming a problem, I turn my hand away from the canvas and think of some beautiful color and use it."

Early Etching, Untitled. Kruse enhanced his printmaking skills at the National Academy of Design.

The Academy provided facilities and materials to support learning experiences involving basic artistic media, including oils, tempera, pastel, etching, lithography, and even sculpture.

Most important of all, enrollment in the Academy afforded an entree into accreditation as an authorized copyist at the Metropolitan Museum of Art. Some of the most valuable educational experiences for the young artist came during the mornings spent producing copies of some of the world's great painting masterpieces. Accredited students were permitted access to the Metropolitan's exhibition halls in the morning, before the museum was opened to the general public. Each student was assigned a locker in which to store an easel, canvases, a folding chair, paints, brushes, and other working materials.

For half of each day when Academy assignments opened access to this paradise, the teen-aged Alex Kruse immersed himself in a heavenly environment of artistic greatness. He took full advantage of the opportunity, exploring the minds, the creative intellects, the palettes, and the brushstrokes of such revered greats as Hals, Rembrandt, Rubens, Bosch, El Greco, and Corot. During this interlude in Kruse's life, these were his teachers; their canvases, his textbooks.

Kruse's later notes describe a memorable encounter that occurred during one of his copying sessions:

...I will always be grateful for having studied with Emil Carlsen.

He suggested we take time out occasionally from Academy study and copy an occasional old master at the Metropolitan Museum. And several of us did: Rembrandt, Frans Hals, . . . and even Wm. M. Chase's *Fish Study*. This last one resulted in a most exciting experience for me. I was about three-fourths completed with the Wm. M. Chase still life of a rusty fish on an oval white dish when a distinguished looking gentleman with a grayish goatee tapped me on the shoulder and introduced himself in the big I and little you fashion. He stood erect and glanced down at me from underneath his pince-nez eyeglasses. Then with an air of dignity and an authoritative tone, he said, "I painted that canvas." I bowed before him. "It's an honor to meet you," I said, "I'm really overwhelmed." (And I actually was).

"Well, my lad, since you're so glad to meet me, I'm going to let you in on the procedure I used to get the slimy quality in that slippery looking fish. It's a very unorthodox method I've used. I obtained that effect by laying in the underlying body color with white enamel out of a can and used Demar Varnish, also out of the can, as a medium. Then I painted right into it, first with the main masses of three dimensional form, then the varied fin accents and snappy touches in the area of the eye, mouth and tail."

This was my happy day. Upon his shaking my hand to say goodbye and good luck, I held his hand long enough to say that Emil Carlsen is my instructor. "Good for you. I just bought one of his paintings."

As the immigrants of the Lower East Side Americanized themselves, increasing numbers worked toward and ultimately applied for citizenship. With citizenship came votes. Given the realities of time and place, politics was an inevitable, pervasive part of the lives of East Siders. On the East Side, political dominance was regarded as a divine right of Tammany Hall, the Democratic juggernaut that ruled the city.

Tammany was in control. Tammany stood for the status quo, and also for a vested interest in keeping voters dependent and subservient. The wisdom of the streets held that "you can count on Tammany when you need a favor." Favors came in the form of jobs, handouts, public picnics on national holidays, and outright cash in exchange for votes; all were part of the way of life.

But not all East Siders were politically docile. Unrest was in the air and many people among the area's poor and exploited found themselves displaying a natural affinity for and attraction to movements that promised fairness, improvement, and equality for all humans. The tides of change were flowing and found voice in a number of movements identified broadly as "isms." Many intellectual and restless denizens of the Lower East Side found themselves exploring the platforms and promises of socialists, communists, and anarchists.

The turmoil in the simmering undercurrents of the cauldron of

18

humanity that was the Lower East Side was stirred provocatively by the ill-fated Kerenski revolt that failed to topple the Russian Czar in 1905. Until then, socialism had been a topic of intense theoretical interest, tempered by the futility from rejection or vicious suppression of any active pursuits of political goals. The Kerenski Revolution was something tangible. It proved to Lower East Side dreamers that there were kindred spirits abroad in the world and that the concepts they espoused could, indeed, become actionable. Kerenski elevated socialist utopian dreams to the level of potential achievability.

Sigmund Kruse was one of the elders among East Side socialists. He was a committed believer before he emigrated from Germany. Throughout Alex's growing-up years, the youngster heard his father abhorring exploitation of workers and advocating forms of government in which common people would take over ownership and control of the means and mechanisms of production. From the time he was a small boy, Alex sat at the fringes of a number of conferences and discussions at which Sigmund hosted bench brother Gompers and other future unionists. Young Alex grew up hearing of and later reading works by or about the likes of Emma Goldman, Eugene V. Debs, and John Reed, all revered leaders of a virile liberalism that attracted participation by a cross section of intellectuals.

Emma Goldman was the fiery anarchist, social conscience, politician, free-love advocate, and pacifist who maintained a flamboyant presence in New York for some three decades. She was deported to her native Russia in 1919 as punishment for her World War I pacifism. After some years of residence in Russia, the outspoken, highly independent Goldman began to write critically about life and politics in the Soviet Union. Her influence on Kruse was strong enough so that copies of Emma Goldman's pamphlets were retained among his personal files throughout his life. Beginning during his teens, Alex Kruse was frequently in attendance at Emma Goldman's lectures, including her frequent appearances at the Ferrer Center (the socialist club where a teen-aged and young-adult Alex Kruse was among the active) as well as at events where she participated in political panels.

Eugene V. Debs came to prominence as organizer, strike leader, and head of the railroad firemen's union. He ran a campaign as Socialist candidate for President of the United States from a federal prison, where he was serving time following conviction on charges trumped up by railroad interests after a strike. Debs, along with Emma Goldman, was a frequent lecturer at the Ferrer Center.

Another star on the left-facing horizon of that era was John Reed, the

Early student sketches. To save money, Kruse often drew multiple images on the same sheet, then turned the paper over and drew more on the other side.

born-to-wealth, Harvard-educated, convert to working people's causes. Reed was a well-spoken zealot who became an on-site participant in the Russian revolution and ultimately became the only American buried in the Kremlin. For Alex Kruse, Reed, was a regular presence within his neighborhood activities. Later, Kruse became active in events at New York's John Reed Club.

As a teenager and later, Alex Kruse also attended meetings of socialist and other liberal organizations at which both political figures and artists he held in high esteem were active participants, including Robert Henri, John Sloan, and George Bellows. These individuals, with whom Alex Kruse enjoyed regular contact during his formative years, all ranked high on the informal honor roll of East Side liberalism.

The Ferrer Center was a hub for all of these goings on. The disillusioned and restless among the growing intellectual community within New York met regularly in the barn-like loft occupied by the Center to drink tea and group-dream of a different world order. In addition to its purely political activities, the Ferrer Center also provided educational and creative opportunities for Kruse when he was fifteen or sixteen and for a few years thereafter. Robert Henri and George Bellows conducted art classes that played an important part in Alex Kruse's continuing education and professional development. Contacts with Henri and Bellows helped bring Kruse into active relationships with a close-knit group whose members became recognized leaders in establishing and expanding a uniquely American brand of artistic social realism.

The artists who led the evolution of this art of social realism—particularly Jerome Myers, Henri, Sloan, and Bellows—were part of a movement which became widely known as the Ash Can School. Some key leaders of the group—Henri, Sloan, and George Luks among them—had their start as newspaper illustrators during an era marked by muckraking exposures of the brutalization of labor and the exploitation of workers pouring into America, particularly from Southern and Eastern Europe. Their art reflected the subjects to which they had previously been sensitized by their occupations as recorders of news. Their drawings and paintings showed the misery in which Lower East Side immigrants subsisted and labored. They illustrated the societal evils which their radical political confederates sought to rectify. Their subject matter ran from rag pickers to pushcart peddlers to sweatshops to bums on park benches to elbow-to-elbow crowding in tenements. Their paintings and drawings told tales of toil and gave voice to the dignity of striving.

Robert Henri was the main catalyst and point man for the social realists prominent in American art circles during the first decades of the twentieth century. By the time he settled in New York in 1900, Henri was well established as a born teacher and artistic stylist, and also as a recognized leader of the American art community. He reached that point following a circuitous route that started in 1865, when he was born as Robert Henry Cozad in Cincinnati, a base from which his father plied his peripatetic trade as a riverboat gambler. In 1872, John Jackson Cozad, Henri's father, took an option from the Union Pacific Railroad on some 50,000 acres of land in eastern Nebraska. He moved the family to this site and established the town of Cozad. The family abandoned the project in 1882 when Cozad shot and killed a man in a dispute.

The family moved to Denver, then gravitated East to Philadelphia, where all the male family members changed their names. Son Robert took the name Robert Earl Henri (pronounced Hen-rye) and also elected to develop the artistic skills that emerged as he grew to manhood by enrolling in the Pennsylvania Academy of Art, which was the most prestigious art school in the country at the time (1886). In 1888, Henri made the first of several trips to Paris, returning to Philadelphia in 1891. The following year, he was hired as a news illustrator at the *Philadelphia Press,* where his co-workers included George Luks, John Sloan, Everett Shinn, and William Glackens, artists whose careers were to be intertwined throughout their lives. Henri, always the natural teacher, tempted the others to attend workshops and philosophic discussions that weaned them away from commercial illustration and into fine art.

By the time he settled in New York in 1900, Henri was a confirmed socialist, an established artist, and a dedicated teacher. He instructed Alex Kruse at informal classes held in the Ferrer Center and later became a strong influence over the young artist at a series of diverse programs in which Alex enrolled, particularly at the Art Students League.

George Bellows, was born in 1880 into a prosperous middle-class family in Columbus, Ohio. He remained in Columbus until his graduation as a business major from Ohio State University. At that point, over the strong objections of his family, he elected to go to New York and become an artist. Henri became his teacher and Bellows became an alter ego and constant companion of Henri. Bellows reached a relatively high level of success as an artist in a short time. He alternated with Henri as an instructor at the informal sessions at the Ferrer Center.

Early Sketches. (1918). The figure on the right is John Sloan. Evidently, Alex Kruse elected to do a quick sketch of his teacher after completing a class assignment.

John Sloan was born in Lock Haven, Pennsylvania, in 1871. Lock Haven was a lumber town which provided raw materials for Sloan family businesses as cabinet makers and undertakers, occupations that went together naturally in those days. When John was five, the family moved to Philadelphia, where John discovered the library at an early age. By the time he was twelve, John had read completely through all the works of Shakespeare and Dickens. This provided a basis for his later emergence as a scholar and philosopher for the group of artist-realists who remained in touch with one another through most of the first half of the twentieth century. In 1904, Sloan became the last of the Philadelphia Four (along with Luks, Glackens, and Shinn) to join Henri in New York. In 1905, when Henri's first wife, Linda, died, John and Dolly Sloan took him in almost as a boarder. Henri and Sloan maintained close connections for many years.

A long-lasting comraderie and mutual commitment grew out of the way Ferrer Center classes were conducted. The effort was totally cooperative. Budgets were established for hiring models, cost of materials, refreshments, and a general contribution to the Center. The instructors donated their time. The students pitched in equal amounts to cover costs.

That arrangement covered the physical and financial aspects of the program. More important in the long run was the aesthetic sharing that took place among all of the instructors and students. They worked in close proximity and dealt with the same basic subject matter. Henri was committed to instruction through demonstration. He and his students shared general beliefs about artistic principles in such areas as treatments of subjects, use of color, composition, and other techniques, while maintaining high degrees of individuality in execution of their own styles. Students benefitted from the shared creativity and commitment of the entire group to both the political ideals of the Ferrer Center and the principle of teaching and learning by following an instructor's demonstrations.

Another socialist institution that attracted young Alex Kruse was the Rand School, where he studied literature, history, and other subjects in addition to attending occasional lectures by Eugene Debs. In 1905, seventeen-year-old Alex Kruse was accorded his first one-man show at the Rand School. The headmaster of this school, only four years older than Kruse, was an early influence who later became a personal friend. The man was Will Durant. During the 1960s, after Alex and Anna Kruse moved to Hollywood, they became close friends of the Durants. Over a period of several years, Ariel Durant breakfasted on bagels and lox at the Kruse apartment several times a week.

Socialism and Ash Can School art became something of a set, nurturing each other during a formative period as New York emerged as an American hub for politics and culture. From today's perspective, it is important to stress that the pursuit of socialism and the other isms of the day was carried on with a mindset that was both naive and idealistic. The ideal of giving labor a voice with which to speak for fair working conditions was seen as worth talking about and fighting for. Only later, when the organizations formed during this era achieved a high level of success, did acquired power distort the ideals and corrupt the people who were involved. By then, however, the founding utopians were off chasing other rainbows. The purity of intent of their ideals and activities at the turn of the twentieth century reflected an honest concern for the welfare and social progress of the poor and mistreated people whose plight they recorded.

National Academy of Design, Class of 1904-1908. Alex Kruse is at the right, rear, near the door.

3
Foundation for a Breakthrough

The Philadelphians who had worked together on the *Press,* on transplanting themselves in New York and getting increasingly serious about their roles in the fine arts, acquired a roguish nickname: they called themselves and became known as "The Black Gang." Ringleader of the gang was Robert Henri, who had gotten the rest involved in a transition from newspaper illustration to serious painting. Other members, often referred to as "The Philadelphia Four," were John Sloan, William Glackens, George Luks, and Everett Shinn.

The ideas—and the work generated—by these five gradually mounted a powerful movement that challenged the established artistic standard that dominated the New York scene at the turn of the century. This establishment was represented and perpetuated by the ultra-literal realism of the National Academy. At the time the Philadelphia Gang set up shop in New York, the National Academy held a virtual monopoly over the art that was considered fit for public viewing.

To be sure, change was in the air. In particular, the French impressionists held a status that could be classified as waiting in the wings. They were in a strong, possibly dominant, position in France. Works by Cezanne, Renoir, Pissaro, Van Gogh, Toulouse-Latrec, Manet, and Monet had begun to cross the Atlantic and were being shown selectively. But it would take the Philadelphia Gang to challenge the dominance of the Academy before the European impressionists, post-impressionists, and nonrepresentational artists could begin to come into their own in America.

Henri, who had been an impressionist and post-impressionist himself during his sojourn in France, set the course for public appearance of an entirely new kind of social realism in art. Later, Alex Kruse, after he was established as a critic, preferred the term "creative realism." At its inception, the group borrowed some of its basic concepts from the naturalistic literature of the day, a movement to which Henri and Sloan were particularly sensitive.

A whole branch of literature had evolved around a mission to expose the ills acquired by society at large under the impetus of the Industrial Revolution. In England, tales of horror emerged from works of Charles Dickens and Thomas Hardy. In France, the torch was carried by Emile Zola. In America, naturalistic literature was stimulated in periodicals by muckrakers like Lincoln Steffens and Ida Tarbell. Novelists like Frank Norris and Upton Sinclair helped produce a body of literary work that heightened public awareness to the plight of the exploited poor.

Of America's naturalist novelists, Theodore Dreiser forged perhaps the closest connection between the literary and graphic arts. One of Dreiser's popular novels was *The Genius*, a book about a brilliant man with broad interests and talents. Popular theories held that either Everett Shinn or John

George Benjamin Luks. The Boxing Match (Oil). (Courtesy of the Virginia Steele Scott Collection, Henry E. Huntington Library and Art Gallery.)

Sloan was the model for Dreiser's hero.

Henri and the Philadelphia Four led the way in introducing the same images of desolation into the graphic arts. As a group, they combined their creative power in rejecting the notion that pictures had to be pretty and/or decorative. They committed to canvas and paper some dramatic, real images of life and times in urban

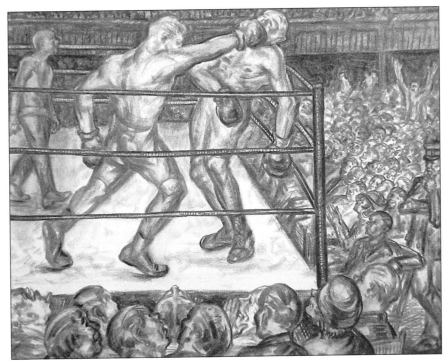

Amateur Bout. (Drawing). During the early 1900s, boxing and wrestling matches provided popular subject matter for several of the Ash Can artists.

America. Their landscapes were the backyards and street markets of the Lower East Side. The impromptu studios where they captured their special views of reality were the sites where meat, vegetables, and other life-supporting sales transactions took place. They rode the elevated trains and streetcars of New York and captured the weariness of their fellow riders.

And they attended the prizefights and wrestling matches that were dominant sporting events of the day as well as entertainment mainstays for the working classes, capturing the intense battles of the gladiators. Alex Kruse often joined Luks, Sloan, Bellows, and others at prizefights and wrestling matches at Manhattan clubs, including Sharkey's. Outstanding examples of art produced between 1904 and 1910 came from these sojourns.

The artistic establishment of the time scoffed at these works, which were held to depict unfit subjects. If any single individual had mounted a campaign to legitimatize reality as art, he (or she) would have been laughed into oblivion. But the five strong, determined gang members and followers accumulated from the ranks of their students (Bellows, Kruse, Reginald Marsh, Rockwell Kent, Guy Pene du Bois, Yasuo Kuniyoshi, Leon Kroll, Peggy Bacon, Gifford Beale, and others) were able to make a difference. The established, respected Jerome Myers also added weight to the movement. Collectors on the New York scene responded to works of art that reflected the life they witnessed in their daily experiences. Public institutions and private galleries began to recognize the legitimacy of the new realism by showing the works of these pioneers.

In 1897, on returning from a stay in Europe, Henri was honored with a one-man show at his alma mater in Philadelphia, the Pennsylvania Academy of Art. The show presented a mixture of subjects, including a number of figure paintings, a genre in which Henri excelled. But almost half the pieces were cityscapes and closeups of city people. The show drew elaborate critical acclaim accompanied by mediocre sales. But this was a beginning. Henri's show gave legitimacy to the new genre and set the stage for him to be joined by Bellows, Sloan, Luks, Glackens, Shinn, and Myers.

Important fallouts from the Academy show in Philadelphia took the form of contacts established between Henri and leading figures in the New York art world. William Merritt Chase was sufficiently impressed to borrow several Henri paintings, which he showed in New York. Of even more lasting consequence was a contact between Henri and William Macbeth, the New York dealer who was to share an important moment of glory with Henri and his friends some years later.

In 1898, Henri returned to Europe, embarking on a grand tour that encompassed France, Spain, and England. He returned to New York in 1901 and resumed contacts that had been initiated following the Pennsylvania Academy show of 1897. Shortly thereafter, Henri accepted an invitation to organize a small group showing at the Allan Gallery. He included works of William Glackens and others as well as his own.

In 1902, Henri was the first of his group to be accorded a one-man show in a dealer's gallery. This was staged by William Macbeth. It played to rave reviews from critics. But only two paintings were sold. However, the net result was to enhance Henri's reputation in art circles and also to increase acceptance of the brand of realism he was pioneering.

In 1903, Everett Shinn, who had had two one-man shows in Paris in 1900, had a one-man show in New York at the Knoedler Galleries.

Building upon his contacts with Macbeth, Henri organized and served as prime mover for a show that has since been recognized as a watershed event in the evolution of American art. In February, 1908, Macbeth opened a massive exhibition for "The American Eight of 1908." This single showing did more than any previous activity to establish acceptance and legitimacy for naturalistic realism in American art. The Eight, all Philadelphia transplants to the New York scene, were Henri, Sloan, George Luks, William Glackens, Everett Shinn, Maurice Prendergast, Arthur B. Davies, and Ernest B. Lawson.

Henri and Sloan are identified and described earlier. Luks is introduced as the man who discovered and encouraged a pre-teen Alex Kruse

28

as he sketched on Grand Street. However, the players in this important scene, other than Henri and Sloan, merit further introduction.

George Luks's personality and lifestyle are reflected realistically in a tale that was one of Alex Kruse's favorite stories about his mentor: When Luks moved from Philadelphia to settle in New York in 1896, he traveled by train to Hoboken, New Jersey, then by ferry to lower Manhattan. After he paid his ferry fare of three cents, Luks discovered that the total remains of his worldly worth was seven cents. Noting that this stake was not even enough to purchase a shot of Irish whiskey at a bar, he threw his remaining capital over the side of the ferry into the Hudson River.

When Luks arrived in New York, it was still early in the morning. He made his way to the offices of the *New York World,* arriving before the staff showed up for work. Luks used the men's room at the *World* to shave and adjust his wardrobe by donning his last clean shirt. When he was finished, he went to the art department to wait for the department head to make his appearance. While he waited, Luks withdrew a pencil stub from his pocket, borrowed several sheets of stationery from a secretary's desk, and rapidly drew sketches of virtually everyone he saw.

Fortunately for Luks, he was a master of the rapid sketch, a skill that stood him in good stead throughout his professional life. He also had a mental agility for glancing at a subject and immediately positioning his source material within a selected image area on paper or canvas. He was naturally left handed. However, he could draw with his right hand as well. Luks also had developed the ability to sketch with both hands simultaneously in executing a drawing. Completed sketches appeared in as little as five minutes.

When the art director arrived, Luks presented his impromptu portfolio. The art director glanced at the sketches, immediately recognizing all of Luks's subjects. Luks was then asked if he could do the same type of work in pen and ink. With his usual modesty, he replied that his pen-and-ink drawings were even better. Luks was hired on the spot and assigned to draw a comic strip, *The Yellow Kid,* whose original artist had just departed. The transaction was completed when Luks drew an advance sufficient to keep himself in whiskey until regular paydays rolled around.

That was the story, one of many that surrounded Luks, most of them subject to skepticism by listeners who got the tales from the man himself or from those who willingly expanded his larger-than-life image. One thing that was certain, however, was Luks's love affair with any whiskey bottle within reach.

Luks was born in 1866 in Williamsport, Pennsylvania, a timing he later described as coinciding with the moment when "our goddamn Congress was trying to bash Andy Johnson out of office." When George was a baby, his father, a doctor, moved the family to Philadelphia, where they lived in a second-story apartment above a drug store that the father also ran.

Growing up, Luks developed an outgoing personality to match his physical agility. He and his brother, Bill, had a professional vaudeville act that lasted for a number of years. There were also stories that had Luks boxing professionally under the name of Chicago Whitey. Stories of this type were hard to confirm, even when Luks was alive; his imagination was simply too vivid and his natural inclination to tell stories that spellbound audiences was insatiable. One fact that is known, however, is that the vaudeville act broke up when Bill left for medical school. At that point, George went off to Europe to study art. The brothers remained close, so much so that Bill was in attendance when George's liver gave out and he died in a New York hospital in 1933.

As a member of The Black Gang and of the wider circle that grew around it, Luks developed a reputation for being unselfish. He was an excellent, dedicated teacher, and, always, an exceptional interpreter of urban life.

Another member of The Black Gang, or the Philadelphia Four, developed the association that led him into the group during his youth. William Glackens was born in Philadelphia to the family of a railroad employee. From early childhood, he showed a natural skill at drawing, a trait that drew him to John Sloan when they were fellow students at Philadelphia's Central High School beginning in 1884.

In his rendition of drawings, Glackens was said to have a mind like a camera. He could glance quickly at a complex landscape, then recall the images in great detail at later dates, sometimes years after the initial visual exposure. This special talent led him naturally into the field of newspaper illustration. In 1891, he was hired as an illustrator at the *Philadelphia Record.* A year later, he was lured to the *Philadelphia Press,* where he joined Henri and the other members of the Philadelphia Four: Sloan, Luks, and Shinn. Like the others, Glackens also studied evenings at the Pennsylvania Academy of Art.

In 1895, Glackens joined Henri on a trip to France, an experience from which, an observer remarked later, he retained more French influence in his art than the other Americans with whom he shared the experience. On returning from France, Glackens joined Luks on the staff of the *New York World,* leaving shortly thereafter to cover the Spanish-American War in Cuba.

Back in New York, Glackens participated, rather than shared leadership, in a number of joint efforts with his Philadelphia compatriots, including a group showing with Sloan and Henri in 1901. When Henri spearheaded the formation of the 1908 Macbeth Galleries showing, Glackens was a natural recipient of an invitation. Observers have characterized his participation as going along with the group rather than leading the trend-setting activity.

In part, a tendency to aloofness by Glackens has been attributed to the fact that his wife, Edith, came from an affluent New Haven family. Edith and their children retained close relationships with her parents. Glackens, influenced by an intense love for his wife, spent comparatively more time with his family than in the social activities of his compatriots from Philadelphia.

The final member of the Philadelphia Four, Everett Shinn, was the most intellectually independent. Shinn was born into a Quaker family in Woodstown, New Jersey. His upbringing affected his later life in diverse ways. For example, he was a teetotaler who was critical of Luks and the other drinkers in the group. In an apparent negative reaction to his background, he married and divorced four wives and also cultivated a taste for elegance both in personal lifestyle and in the subject matter of many of his paintings. Shinn did draw and paint Ash Can type views of New York Streets. But he also devoted a substantial portion of his artistic efforts to rendering images of uptown theaters, music halls, and society subjects.

Judgments of Shinn from within the art world hold that he lacked dedication to and focus upon his art. There were periods of years within his life during which he gave up painting entirely, opting to focus on jobs in newspaper or magazine illustration. His diversity has been illustrated by the project that saw him building his own theater in New York's Waverly Place. Originally, the purpose of the building was to create a facility where he could work on large segments of a mural he had been commissioned to do for the State House in Trenton, New Jersey. Along the way, Shinn decided, as long as he had a suitable place, to produce plays. He went ahead with thirty-five productions before the project was abandoned.

Shinn's natural detachment helped to make him perhaps the most incisive commentator about fellow members of The American Eight. He was known to believe that the group and its members lacked a positive artistic focus; that their efforts were directed instead as opposing forces against the literal, rigid style adhered to by the National Academy.

The main constant in Everett Shinn's career was his ability to render sketches quickly, accurately, and with excellent quality. It was said that he was faster even than the ambidextrous Luks, who could draw with both hands concurrently. He was always in demand as an illustrator and appeared to be tempted by the many offers he received, willing to put off or ignore his career as a fine artist in favor of short-term challenges.

The remaining three members of The American Eight—Maurice Prendergast, Ernest Lawson, and Arthur B. Davies—participated in the show primarily as friends of Henri and the Philadelphia Four rather than through an affinity for the urban realism, or "Ash Can" subject matter or painting style, as it was dubbed by critics. In addition to the bonds of friendship established through the Pennsylvania Academy of Art and later encounters that included sharing of studios, a shared antipathy to the rigidity of the National Academy provided a common cause.

Prendergast is generally considered to have followed a post-impressionist style that reflected his work in France, where he was influenced strongly by the work of other post-impressionists, such as Cezanne and Seurat.

Lawson's work was also influenced strongly by his French experience. In 1893, he shared a Paris studio with W. Somerset Maugham and is believed to have been the model for a character in Maugham's book, *Of Human Bondage*. His work shows definite impressionist influences, with no inclination to share subject matter with the Ash Can School adherents. (Alex Kruse always credited Henry McBride with origination of the term "Ash Can" to describe the work of urban realists. Others attribute the term to different observers. It is agreed, however, that the term was in use before the 1908 exhibition of The American Eight.)

Davies' work shows a blend of realism based on remembered landscapes from his youth in upper New York State and the kind of fantasy that led him to show a group of unicorns in one of his best-known paintings. However, Davies was a recognized craftsman with the stature to gain him admission to the National Academy. He also held a position of respect that made him the logical choice to be the organizer and implementer of the massive Armory Show of 1913, the event credited with making abstract art acceptable and respectable in the United States and of catapulting nonrepresentational art to a position of dominance that lasted for decades.

At one level, the groundbreaking Macbeth show of 1908 resulted from William Macbeth's commitment to what had become known as Ash Can art. At another level, show participation resulted from a buddy system that had Robert Henri at its hub.

Some natural basis for conflict between William Macbeth and Henri as leader of the Philadelphians evolved around Macbeth's strong belief that Jerome Myers was the real pioneer of Ash Can painting. In some measure, time and experience supported Macbeth's position: the Philadelphia Eight never exhibited again as a unified group. On the other hand, the identity and acceptance of Ash Can art gained both momentum and acceptance following the 1908 show.

Although existing historical literature takes little or no note of Macbeth's strategy, the fact is that he held two concurrent exhibitions in February, 1908. Alex Kruse observed the preparations for and conduct of the 1908 Macbeth exhibition personally and from a close-up, inside perspective. The following comment from a Kruse notebook entry in 1969 includes information and observations that may be published here for the first time:

> Robert Henri, as an instructor, was influential in encouraging and developing more great talents in contemporary American art than anyone could give an honest accounting of.
>
> Let us start with Henri the artist first. He was a student at the Pennsylvania Academy in Philadelphia of Thomas Anshutz and Thomas Eakins, two American masters about whose art there is no doubt as to their sincerity, integrity, knowledgeability of craft and distinct individuality. Anshutz stressed the importance of knowing the muscles and bones underneath the skin. He was a fine colorist. At the Pennsylvania Academy, he [Henri] met up with such promising younger students as George Luks, William Glackens, Maurice Prendergast, Ernest Lawson, John Sloan, Arthur B. Davies, and Everett Shinn. John Sloan admitted to me [Alex Kruse] that he studied in the Pennsylvania Academy in the antique drawing class for only six months. But he took a shine to the leadership of Robert Henri and the big-brother type of his studio dialogs with that group of his younger friends who, in later years, developed into the "American Eight of 1908."
>
> The 1908 exhibition was their first and last collective group show sponsored by the far-sighted William Macbeth of the well known Macbeth Galleries. Macbeth had but one regret, and it was why Jerome Myers was not included in that group. Therefore, to even things out without controversy, Macbeth assigned an adjoining gallery for a one-man show for Jerome Myers' paintings. It seems fair to assume that Mr. Macbeth realized that even though no artist has a monopoly on subject matter, at least one might say Jerome Myers was the daddy of them all when it comes to human interest subject matter that existed in New York's Lower East Side at the turn of the century.

As noted in Chapter 1, Alex Kruse observed the birth of Ash Can art first-hand when he studied under Myers at the Educational Alliance. Kruse was a direct observer as Myers used street people of the Lower East Side as subjects for paintings produced as early as 1900, at a point in time before all members of The Eight were assembled in New York.

4
Turning Point

The exhibition of The Eight, which took place in February, 1908, was an immediate and unqualified critical success, even though actual sales of paintings were comparatively meager. Immediately, the new realism was the center of attention in the art world, establishing a place that set it apart and, in some minds, above the position occupied by the classical realism practiced at the Academy.

The success of the Macbeth show startled the staid members of the Academy, who reacted quickly with an action clearly intended to put the upstart Eight in their place. The directors of the Academy invited The Eight to show the paintings from the Macbeth exhibition in the Academy's 1908 annual exhibition. The establishment members clearly believed that the new paintings of social realism would suffer so badly by comparison with the classic works by Academy members that the public would laugh the Ash Can painters out of existence.

The opposite happened. The Ash Can realists stole the show, critically and in terms of public acceptance. Through this one event, new standards for artistic values were created. In the process, New York also emerged as a world-class center of artistic activity.

The Macbeth show and the leaders of The Eight had a major impact in shaping the artistic values and directions of Alexander Kruse's life. The exhibition coincided with Alex Kruse's twentieth birthday. The event brought him into close, inspirational, idealism-sharing contact with world-class creative giants, the innovative artistic leaders of his day. The exhibiting artists themselves were much older than Kruse, some old enough to be his father, others almost old enough.

In the light of developments that followed, this difference in age may turn out to have been highly significant. A number of art historians and critics have expressed the belief that the realists among The Eight peaked in both influence on the artistic world and in personal talent levels at or within a few years after the Macbeth show. Certainly, as is shown in pages that follow, the career decisions of the realists following the critical success of 1908 did little or nothing to enhance their collective reputation or to add to the position of social realism in the overall scheme of things within the art world. Within five or six years, there were new trends which some (including Alex Kruse) called fads.

The point is that despite public acceptance of Ash Can painting—along with the vigor of paintings of cityscapes and city people—early adherents to the Ash Can school (especially the members of the Philadelphia Gang) appear to have plateaued professionally or even gone in a downhill direction following this moment of glory. They tended to experiment with color and composition theories (described below), thus separating themselves from the initial inspiration that led to fame and placed them in the public spotlight during the single instant in history centered around the Macbeth show and its immediate aftermath. This reference about peaking of reputations is about the Ash Can painters only—Henri and the Philadelphia Four. Davies enhanced his reputation in the years following the 1908 Macbeth show through his activities as head of the organization that staged the Armory Show in 1913. Prendergast prospered as impressionism was imported to and gained wide acceptance in America.

Alex Kruse reacted differently to the trends that emerged following the show of 1908. He remained true to his subject matter and his commitment to American content throughout his life. This could have occurred because of his youth in 1908 as compared with the midlife status of his teachers, mentors, and political compatriots among the close-knit group of which he was a member. For Alex Kruse, subjects of social realism were still part of a discovery process. For his older teachers and mentors, it may have seemed that the time was right to look for different materials and methods.

Among the influences that diverted at least some members of The Eight from the spontaneous vigor that was vital to their initial appeal were new theories about color and composition that emerged in 1910 and 1913. Henri and his close friend Bellows were particularly influenced by these theoretical principles, Sloan to a somewhat lesser degree. Ultimately, conceptual and intellectual differences emerged between Henri and Bellows on the one hand and Sloan, Luks, and others (Kruse among them) on the other.

The color theories that impacted contemporary painters around 1910 and for some time thereafter were enunciated by Hardesty Gillmore Maratta, a Chicago artist and art theorist. Maratta's theories purported to establish relationships, or essential connections, between the colors on an artist's palettes that corresponded with the tonal values of a musical composition. He prescribed a balance of colors he felt to be mandatory in every painting. Maratta's influence was particularly strong among the abstract and other nonobjective artists who were emerging in his day. Henri became enthusiastic about this methodology, applying it to his work, particularly figure paintings, and to his writing about creative and artistic theories. In retrospect, the effect upon Henri's painting seems to have been to stabilize and remove some of the spontaneous quality and revolutionary feeling that marked his pre-1908 style that was based upon his emotional reaction to observed color and upon the compositional traits natural to his subjects. A possible positive effect was that the Maratta palette did diminish Henri's tendency to create paintings with dark tonal values.

A series of composition theories were added to Maratta's color schemes by Jay Hambridge, who labeled his new design theories as Dynamic Symmetry. Hambridge's theories attributed mathematical proportions to effective composition, theoretically as adaptations of principles observed in Greek and Roman art. Structured mathematical frameworks were to be superimposed over and to control the placement of elements within an artistic composition. Critics have asserted that compositions are just as effective when creative innovators rely on their natural instincts and that Hambridge-inspired compositions are contrived and artificial.

Although they remained devoted friends, Sloan and Henri evolved intellectual differences after Henri accepted and subscribed to the theories of Maratta and Hambridge.

Unfortunately, some art historians and later critics have attributed both undue and inappropriate influences upon artistic works to the Maratta and Hambridge theories, even among artists who ultimately embraced these techniques. An example was observed during 1993 at a showing in the Los Angeles County Museum of Art of a traveling exhibit of the work of George Bellows. At a slide show purporting to explain the works on display, and in docent tours of the works themselves, examples of Maratta and Hambridge principles were cited in connection with a Bellows painting of a fight night at Sharkey's and paintings done on the Lower East Side. A number of the paintings to which Maratta and Hambridge influences were attributed were produced prior to 1910, the year in which Maratta's theories were introduced.

Alex Kruse didn't subscribe to the artificial rules put forward during his formative years. He practiced intuitive methods he liked to refer to as "creative realism." That is, he insisted that the artist had an obligation to take elements found in nature or in scenes played before him and arrange them in logical patterns that conveyed both viewing pleasure and, in some instances, a message of import, to the viewer.

Kruse commented specifically on the stylistic constraints of the Hambridge systems in loose notes found among journal entries for the late 1960s:

> Henri had developed a certain way of painting eyes, a nose, and an ear. The formation and action of hair alignment were in keeping with the expression of the features upon the head, [also] the characteristic with which the head sets on the neck and shoulders and torso.
>
> He advised [students] to develop a sense of proportion in drawing and painting the human figure so that people who are looking for academic perfection will credit you with being a good draftsman.
>
> I'm now beginning to realize that this sort of methodism [the Hambridge composition technique] is apt to run too much into formula. From many years of teaching, he [Henri] developed an academism of his own. Another formula of his was to encourage students in the economy of effort and [to] be content with sketchily grasping the idea and meaning of the action and movement of a figure. This is desirable, of course, but I later realized the importance of self-correction in afterthought...that there are bones and muscles underneath the figures. In order to inculcate some knowledgeability into your art, it is important to become knowledgeable about human anatomy. Calling upon that understanding is better than calling upon a friend for constructive criticism. There was much I found myself unlearning through my studio workshop trials and errors.
>
> Another academic theory of a lecturer on artistic anatomy—and this proved helpful when thoroughly understood—was the advice about figure drawing and painting, namely to wise it up by accenting the temple bones, the cheek bones, the main neck muscles, the collar bones, the elbow location, wrist bones, and joints of the fingers. Watch out for the direction lines of the hip and

the cage of the ribs, the main connecting muscle between the hips and kneecap, and the indentations of the kneecap. Also be mindful of the bones of the arm and the two bones in the forearm, as well as the thighbone attached to the kneecap, which connects the two bones of the leg, which terminate into visible ankles, at which point there articulates the bones of the foot in definite proportions.

I found out that this cannot be schemed over quickly or sketchily…one has first to resort to a graphic recording of the inspiration of any idea. Secondly, [it is important] not to paint or draw according to any knowledge, but to apply that knowledge after the first impression is graphically organized.

There is more to creative drawing and painting than meets the academic eye. Creative intuition does not come in ready-made tubes of paint. The artist must not be afraid to add to his work some elements that he doesn't actually see but that he feels about what he sees. That is why many willing art lovers often don't see what they are looking at. Alertness in art appreciation can become quite enjoyable when the art collector acquires the sympathetic understanding of the aims and aspirations of the artist in any media.

The artist learns by doing as does the writer or composer. So does the art collector. Self-deception and vanity have no place in the field of enjoyable endeavor…

Memory and imagination play important parts in my painting. Both [are] vital mental ingredients of creative interaction. After craft, skill is available at one's fingertips; a dynamic pictorial composition becomes a matter of not merely how to do it, but primarily what you are doing.

When the initial inspiration is clear in the mind, the creative elements seem to be falling into their proper places of person, place, and thing—animate and inanimate. Improvisational composition seems constantly to keep me on the alert. Simplification or elimination [of pictorial elements can] help emphasize balance between the point of interest and the counterpoint of space and shape.

Tackle the difficult part of your painting first—that is, after the composition idea has been laid out. Then, any area that is not coming out as you intended, scrape it out with your palette knife and begin anew, on a trial-and-error basis. Thereby, the effect of spontaneity is attained.

Kruse viewed the Maratta color system differently, as indicated in the following excerpt from his diaries:

> John Sloan's assignments of color experiments based upon the Maratta theory of colors he manufactured proved very helpful. That was a short demonstration lecture series which proved helpful for the rest of my painting days. The class consisted of advanced art students at the time.

Separately, Kruse noted that he approved of the effect of the Maratta system on Henri's work: he felt that the Maratta palette imparted an overall lighter tone to Henri's paintings, which had tended to be on the dark side in his earlier years.

In other diary notes, Kruse comments on his own work inspirations and methods:

> Robert Henri pointed to a plaster cast replica of Michaelangelo's head of Brutus and said "If I were drawing this head I would strive for the there-ness of it."
>
> I took a second look and I became conscious of the shadows, half tones and light areas of the underlying related planes of the forms which were part of the three-dimensional bulk of the overall form. And over the years, whenever I resort to painting from memory or imagination, I apply my awareness of the there-ness of the three-dimensional aspect of the person, place, or thing to be expressed…
>
> Since I have not been painting out-of-doors recently, I find it stimulating to take short walks during the early morning hours. This experience makes me feel better fit physically for my day's painting at the easel indoors for the rest of the day.
>
> Because of a temporary ailing leg, I find it necessary to take brief rests at short intervals. At such times, I sit at some nearby cement-block ledge. I've grown used to the frequent smog weather which now and again intrudes upon sunshine. This situation does not obstruct reminiscences which flow through my mind while I'm comfortably relaxing in the all too frequent sunless air.
>
> At the spur of this moment, a thought occurred to me about how I can best project a feeling of the existence of light, by means of color, within the framework of the canvas I'm working on currently.
>
> Such mentally aesthetic excursions often entail a welcomed string of do's and don't's in the process of self-correction. That includes a consideration of indiscernible fragments of qualities which lead to a better balanced composition. This, in turn, enhances my original inspiration and mental perception. After such brief walks, I return to my work increasingly inspired.

After four years at the National Academy, Alex Kruse, at twenty, had acquired the technical and mechanical tools of the artist's craft. He understood how to create images on paper, copper, litho stone, and canvas. But he also recognized that he had more work to do in establishing a creative rationale to direct his work. He was at a stage he later described as "hand and eye" rendition of images. He wanted to be able to control the composition of his own works rather than having to rely on nature to arrange the elements of his pictures for him.

Kruse also devised an approach that enabled him to expand his teaching activities and still leave him time for his own painting:

> After two years at the Academy, I discovered there would be an examination for Teachers of Art Study in the Summer School

System of the Board of Education. I hurried to the Board office on 59th & Park Ave. and found I had just the required qualification: "Two years' experience in teaching, a high school graduation or its equivalent, and two years of Art School Training"

The exams consisted of a written exam on pedagogics in which Dr Herman Friedel, principal [Davidson School], briefed Prof. Morris Raphael Cohn, [who] briefed me. That was followed a few days later by a test in drawing and watercolor and shortly after came the oral exam conducted by the Board Head, Miss Whitney, and two…teachers. I passed and the experience was a pleasant adventure in a Rivington St. School hours 9-12.

I took my paint box with me every morning and by 1 o'clock I had already gobbled up my sandwich and fruit and taken the West End Line at Brooklyn Bridge to the last stop, New Lots Road.

There was a swampy sort of farm there with about 100 head of cattle. The area resembled views of Holland. It even had a dilapidated windmill. Farther out there was a slimy body of water and…sailboats. My fellow classmate and friend, Ben Benn, had rented the use of a room in a vacant shack used for storage and fodder. The rent was $5 a month. Another student and I paid one dollar each for the privilege of leaving our canvases there. That reduced Benn's rental fee. Somehow the sunsets were just begging to be painted. I'd come home by 9 p.m. and found [sic] an appetizing supper which my devoted mother prepared for her one and only and my father would read the current events out loud for the three of us. My parents always joined me in dessert.

So for the third and fourth year at the Academy I was well fixed for the summers and continued on with my weekend jobs during the fall and winter.

In 1908, I copied at the Metropolitan Museum—Rembrandt, Hals, Corot—and to my surprise Museum visitors used to buy them not only from me but Paul Burlin [sic], Wm. Zorach, Ben Kopman, and several other of my fellow students.

Between copies, I'd wander off to Central Park and Bronx Park and paint landscapes. To my great surprise I found a market for them many years later.

To pursue the creative development he felt he needed, he sought help from artists who had already provided much of his motivation and inspiration. Henri, Luks, and Sloan had all affiliated themselves with the Art Students League during the years in which Kruse was matriculating at the National Academy. So, while he still relied on other vocational activities for physical sustenance, he enrolled at the Art Students League to promote his creative development.

Functionally, Kruse's study at the Art Students League provided learning and working experiences that more closely resembled the best traditions of an apprenticeship than the teacher-student discipline of a traditional school. Kruse and fellow students experienced total immer-

John Sloan Art Class, 1918. (Oil). In addition to Kruse, students include Yasuo Kuniyoshi, Reginald Marsh, Otto Soglow, Peggy Bacon and Tasha Shemitz.

sion in an environment that involved professional tutelage by dedicated instructors and the formation of a close-knit community of students committed to achievement of the same purposes as their leaders. Some of the students maintained friendships throughout their lives, recalling shared incidents of youth long after they moved on into their middle years. Included in this group were Rockwell Kent, Yasuo Kuniyoshi, Leon Kroll, Abraham Walkowitz, Peggy Bacon, Reginald Marsh, Lena Gurr, and the Sawyer brothers.

On many occasions, the easy familiarity that teachers and students evolved with one another was reflected in the paintings they produced at various times. A number of the artists produced portraits of one another: Henri painted Luks and produced a number of drawings and paintings depicting Sloan; Bellows painted Henri; and Kruse produced paintings of a Luks figure class, pencil drawings of Henri and Sloan, and later, portraits of Abraham Walkowitz and Louis Eilshemius. Much later, Kruse did a pastel portrait of Diego Rivera. To describe his experience in developing the portrait of Rivera, Kruse would explain that it was based on a sketch prepared at a Rivera lecture when the artist was in New York in the early 1930s doing the ill-fated Rockefeller Center mural commission. (Management covered over the mural and commissioned a new work because Rivera included a picture of Lenin in the composition.) Kruse would pantomime and describe Rivera's actions as he lumbered up to the speaker's table, raised his massive stomach, rested it on the table, then proceeded with his lecture.

It was also common for the artists of this group to include their cohorts in paintings that included the use of figures. As one example, the Virginia Steele Scott Gallery of American Art at the Huntington Library and Art Collections in Pasadena, California, includes one of a series that Sloan painted at McSorley's Saloon, located off Cooper Union Square in New York City. The piece is entitled *McSorley's Cats*. The red-headed proprietor is off to the right of the composition feeding the cats that were regular denizens of the establishment. The men in the painting (women were not permitted in McSorley's until the 1960s) included Sloan himself, along with easily recognizable figures of Reginald Marsh, George Luks, Yasuo Kuniyoshi, and Alex Kruse.

As the League experience extended, and Kruse remained to take graduate classes after he finished the basic study sequence, his affinity, admiration, and intellectual kinship with John Sloan blossomed and became a major influence on his development as an artist, political personae, and as a human being. In part, the closeness occurred as Kruse concentrated increasingly on printmaking, a medium that also held great attraction for Sloan.

To illustrate the closeness that ensued between mentor and pupil, Alex and Anna Kruse had planned to name their son, born in 1925, John Sloan Kruse. The child's name was changed to Benedict only because Mrs. Kruse's father died suddenly about eight months before the child was born.

Political viewpoints also contributed to the bonding. Kruse, the devoted socialist, drew close to Sloan during the years when the older man served as art editor of *The*

John Sloan. McSorley's Cats. (Oil). Sloan is at lower left with glasses and pipe. Kruse is in center, holding cane. (Courtesy of the Virginia Steele Scott Collection, Henry E. Huntington Library and Art Gallery.

Masses, a literary and artistic journal of the far left. At the time *The Masses* started publication in 1911, Kruse was still a graduate student at the League. He assisted Sloan with publication duties. In retrospect, *The Masses* is recognized as having attracted major talents and produced some important writings and illustrations. Max Eastman, the editor, attracted many eloquent essayists. But he recognized the appeal of illustrations in delivering messages and allowed adequate space for drawings from the leading lights of the art world. Contributing artists included Rockwell Kent, George Bellows, Robert Henri, Arthur B. Davies, Boardman Robinson, Stuart Davis, Jo Davidson, John Barber, and Mahonri Young. *The Masses* ceased publication in 1917, partly in response to the Russian Revolution.

After World War I and during the era when many Americans interpreted the Russian Revolution as a hopeful development, a new publication, *The New Masses,* attempted to satisfy a perceived need for a new literary and artistic voice from the left. By this time, Alex Kruse had matured and gained enough recognition to step in as art editor for *The New Masses.* The editor, Stanley Burnshaw, a poet and essayist, became a close friend of the Kruses during the 1920s through the 1940s, sharing several summer vacations and collaborating on a book project described later.

The Art Students League promoted friendships. The professional and career implications of such friendships are alluded to above. But life was far from being all work and no play at the League. Boys were boys, even then. Many of the male students followed the most popular spectator sports of the day: boxing and wrestling. Alex Kruse, who was shorter and stockier than most of his fellow students, used to explain that his prowess as a wrestler stemmed from the fact that he perspired profusely. Once he worked up a sweat, he would explain with appropriate motions, he could simply slip out of any hold applied by his adversary.

Memories also lingered for Kruse about one gala April Fool's Day while he was a student at the League. One wag squirted prodigious amounts of red paint on all the door knobs in the building, then stood back and went into fits of laughter as the paint showed up on various parts of the anatomies of the unsuspecting.

To top even this dirty trick, a group of the more mischievous students obtained a wide piece of lumber, fastened it over the urinals in the men's room and lettered the inscription "Board of Control" across the obstacle.

5
Moving Uptown

Today, hearing the very name of the uptown Manhattan neighborhood called Harlem conjures up images of a devastated area in a constantly deteriorating state of decay and destruction. This image must be dispelled to recognize that, while Alex Kruse was carrying on his studies at the Art Students League, his parents finally saw their way clear, partly with his help, to leave the Lower East Side and move to the comparative opulence that was attracting many thousands of families from lower Manhattan to the fast-developing uptown area north of Central Park called Harlem.

This, basically, was how New York grew to become the most populous city in the country. Subways and elevated lines were extended into areas that were open farmland or were only lightly developed. Once the transportation was in place, developers were attracted to available and reasonably priced land. The proliferating banks offered attractive terms that enabled families to buy private homes on credit or to afford to rent and furnish larger, more comfortable apartments than those they vacated in lower Manhattan tenements.

The upgrade for the Kruse family was facilitated in part by the fact that Alex was adding enough to the family income to warrant payment of higher rent. The residential buildings being constructed in Harlem were in a vanguard of a trend that marked the spreading out of New York City to accommodate its continually increasing population. Transportation came first. In the case of Harlem, elevated railways—the Second Avenue El, then the Third Avenue El—ran from lower Manhattan into the upper reaches of the island and on into The Bronx. The then-modern New York subway system also came into being starting in the late 1880s and accelerated expansion early in the twentieth century. The Interborough Rapid Transit (IRT) system included subway lines along Lexington Avenue and Seventh Avenue to serve Harlem, along with a Broadway line that ran to the Upper West Side and the area known as Washington Heights.

The living facilities and conditions were luxurious by comparison with the tenement at 133 Henry Street. New-found luxuries included hot running water in the apartment itself, central steam heat, gas stoves instead of coal stoves for cooking, and, most convenient of all, a bathroom right in the apartment.

For a developing artist, Harlem also offered access to many new and different subjects that were worth capturing on paper and canvas. Alex Kruse had already built an impressive portfolio of drawings from his work at Oscar Hammerstein's theater. Nearby in the new Harlem neighborhood, Alex Kruse discovered and gloried in the mixed racial makeup of local entertainment. He and his sketch pad were in fairly frequent attendance at the Cotton Club and other nightspots that dotted One Hundred Twenty-fifth Street. Kruse produced a number of drawings from these venues, one of which was used as the basis for a widely exhibited lithograph entitled *In East Harlem*.

Among the unique experiences related to the upward mobility repre-

In East Harlem. (Lithograph).

sented by the move to Harlem was a charcoal figure drawing, later used as a basis for a lithograph, entitled *Young Smoker*. The subject, shown in profile, is a young man in his late teens lighting a pipe. The lithograph has been shown widely and has been critically acclaimed for its empathetic treatment of the subject.

The subject for this work was the son of the woman who worked as janitress for the building in which the Kruses lived. In recalling the experience, Alex Kruse said that the youngster had been an excellent model. So Alex paid him a dime for his services, earning a scolding from the young man's mother who said that a nickel would have been more than enough and she didn't want her son spoiled in this way. That incident occurred some time between 1910 and 1915.

A *Young Smoker* lithograph was included in a showing held in the late 1960s in the Grand Central area. Kruse had agreed to the exhibit at the urging

Young Smoker. (Lithograph). This print was widely acclaimed. The model returned in later years with his own unique, success story!

of David Brenner, a close family friend who operated a tax-accounting office in a heavy-traffic, street-access location. One of the viewers who wandered into the Brenner exhibit gravitated immediately to the lithograph of the *Young Smoker*. He was an elderly person, about seventy as it turned out, accompanied by a young lady. The man introduced himself to Alex and drew immediate recognition when he was identified as the subject of the lithograph.

As the old acquaintances reminisced, the overpaid model revealed that he had just retired after many years as a judge of the Superior Court. The young woman who accompanied him was his granddaughter. He purchased the print as a gift for her.

The move to Harlem also led Alex Kruse to explore new opportunities for landscape painting. Northern Manhattan represented a whole new world. Among the locations that attracted Kruse were Spuyten Duyvil (Dutch for Spitting Devil), the area in northernmost Manhattan bordering on the Harlem River and looking over toward The Bronx. The subways also provided access to the still-wild Bronx Park area. Streetcars offered

Spuyten Duyvil. (Lithograph).

fast, convenient access to the countryside in Queens, which sits at the end of Long Island, an area of rolling farmland during this period. Even closer at hand was Central Park, used extensively for picnics, games, and as a location where New Yorkers could still breathe comparatively fresh air.

Other changes in Alex's life at this time are described in later reminiscent notes:

In 1909 I started an art class at the YMHA when it was about one-third the present size it is now. I got the job by taking a few of my canvases under my arm together with my summer school teacher credentials to the director and he thought an art class to be a good idea.

By the end of 1910, Dr. Schulman, in charge of Adult Education, came into my class to tell me that my classes will discontinue...So I was left with 22 pupils on my hands. It just so happened that I had already had a sizable studio on 125th St. It was in a discarded Horton Icecream bldg. and I was averaging about one portrait a month. My rental was $10 a month, and that included light and heat, and a sizable place it was. At a ridiculous monthly fee, the students joined my evening class and I was operating rent free.

I kept that up till 1912, when I became very much displeased with the conduct of my portrait art patrons. I decided to take a job with the John Young Scenic Studios. How'd I go about it? I enrolled for the Geo Bridgman course of anatomy lectures. He was head of figure painting at that Studio. I showed him some of my work, told him my need of a steady job. "Come up to see me at the Studio and I'll introduce you to John Young."

During the 2 1/2 years that followed, there were dull months during which we were laid off—which of course I welcomed. It was an opportunity to paint on my own with a vengeance.

Among other advantages, the subway and elevated lines brought cleanliness to urban transportation. The subways and el trains operated on electricity, a vast improvement over the soot-belching steam locomotives of the previous period. At this time also, automobiles and crude trucks were beginning to replace horse-drawn carriages and delivery wagons. This trend was seen as contributing greatly to the sanitation of the city; in 1908, the sanitation department was scooping up and disposing of some twelve tons of horse manure each day.

New York was growing, moving toward its destiny as a world center of commerce and finance. In those days prior to income taxes, the growing number of newly rich moguls could afford to vie with one another in search of good works to be contributed to the community. Libraries, museums, opera, concert halls, and theaters drove a movement that ultimately stimulated the grimy

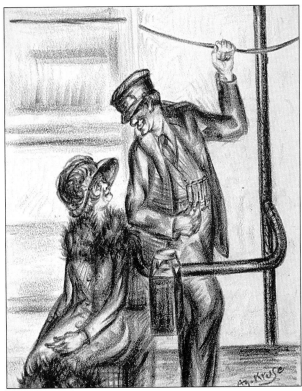

Visiting Travelers. (Drawing). On moving to Harlem, Alex Kruse found himself spending considerable time on elevated and subway trains. His sharp eye and wit were put to good use.

world of tenements and sweat shops to transform itself, at least in part, to a community with cultural advantages for both native New Yorkers and transplants from elsewhere in America or from Europe seeking intellectual stimulation.

In this respect, Alex Kruse found himself living in the right place, at the right time. For Kruse, New York represented home, opportunity, and continuing inspiration because the rapid rate of change became a constant source of new visions and provided infinite varieties of subject matter. This may be a reason why Kruse kept returning to the source materials of his youth whereas people raised in other parts of the country or the world were more prone to seek new areas and new subjects in their later years, partly by creating and seeking artists' colonies in rural locales.

Ice Man. (Oil).

Window Cleaners. (Oil, 16"x12").

6
Organizing an Artistic Mob Scene

One of the effects of the 1908 show at the Macbeth Gallery was to break the longtime grip on American artistic standards and styles—some thought of it as a stranglehold—held by the National Academy of Design. The Ash Can artists struck out for realism in subject matter coupled with flexibility and innovation in artistic expression. As things turned out, the Macbeth show was a first blow in what developed into a battle that persisted for the next five years, culminating with the Armory Show of 1913. When that colossal event was over, the Academy was no longer the dominant arbiter of tastes and standards in the New York art world. But The Eight and their allies who provided the stimulus of opposition also were diminished as a result of the ongoing drive toward modernism.

One of the lines of continuity from the Macbeth show toward the triumph of modern art came from the already-established rebels, Henri and his friends. In 1909, they enlarged upon their circle and started planning for what was to become the largest exhibition of American art to date. They formed the Independent Artists of America, rented space, and staged the Exhibition of Independent Artists in 1910.

Nucleus for the new show consisted of all the members of The Eight, except for Luks, who had a one-man show of his own in preparation. Again, Henri was the leader, working with organizational assistance from Sloan, Davies, Walt Kuhn, and Walter Pach. By this time, young Alex Kruse was ready to become a factor in forming acceptable trends in American realism. He was an early, active member of and a regular exhibitor with the Independents. All Independents shows were open and unjuried, the largest undertaking of that type up to that moment. The first show in 1910 presented 260 paintings, 219 drawings, and a number of sculptures.

Again, public response and critical acclaim were overwhelming; financial response less so. A note in Sloan's diary indicates that attendance was so great that police had to be called in to control the crowds.

The Independents show remained an all-American endeavor that continued as an annual event for decades. During the same period, however, a movement was born to bring trendy modern paintings from Europe, particularly France, into the New York scene. A pioneer in this movement that was to change the direction of American art was Alfred Stieglitz. Ever an individualist and innovator, Stieglitz, already one of the world's leading photographers, split with the august New York Camera Club in 1902. Stieglitz started what became a new movement in photography. He and his followers called themselves Photo-Secessionists, adopting the name from a modern art group in Europe that was breaking away from the impressionists and post-impressionists with nonobjective art forms, including cubism, abstractionism, and surrealism.

In collaboration with Edward Steichen, Stieglitz opened a gallery in 1905, giving it a name taken from its address, the 291 Fifth Avenue Gallery. Stieglitz's gallery was also known informally as the secessionist gallery. At first, exhibits were confined to works of avant garde photography. Then, in 1907, Steichen wrote to Stieglitz from Europe suggesting that they hold an exhibition of drawings by the popular sculptor, Auguste Rodin. Fifty-eight Rodin drawings were accorded indifferent public reaction at a showing in 1908. Undaunted, Stieglitz followed a few months later with an exhibition of drawings by Henri Matisse.

Stieglitz, often with Steichen's help, persevered. The 291 Fifth Avenue Gallery premiered United States showings of the works of European artists who have since become recognized as giants of the modern art movement. Included, in addition to Rodin and Matisse, were Cezanne, Picasso, Toulouse-Lautrec, Henri Rousseau, Georges Braque, and Constantin Brancusi. Works by American innovators who gained early recognition in a 1910 exhibition at the 291 Fifth Avenue Gallery featuring "Young American Painters" included Arthur Dove, Marsden Hartley, John

Marin, Alfred Maurer, Georgia O'Keefe, Abraham Walkowitz, and Max Weber. Among other results, Stieglitz later married Georgia O'Keefe.

Although the 291 Fifth Avenue Gallery launched most of its pioneering exhibits at a time when Alex Kruse was still a student, the young artist was an eager visitor and observer. Kruse also struck up an acquaintance with Stieglitz that eventually led to collaboration. Years later, as art director for a large photoengraving firm, Kruse supervised preparation of illustrations for a number of books and catalogs for Stieglitz, who also became owner of several Kruse works. For young Alexander Kruse, these involvements served, in effect, as profitable and instructive extracurricular student activities.

The revolutionary art event that became the renowned Armory Show had its germination at a show in another innovating New York Gallery. In 1911, the Madison Gallery was established in part of a decorating facility, the Coventry Studios, located at 305 Madison Avenue. The gallery was run by Mrs. Clara S. Davidge. Mrs. Gertrude Vanderbilt Whitney was reputed to be a backer.

In December of 1911, the Madison Gallery held an exhibition for the Pastellists, featuring works in that medium by four established American artists—Jerome Myers, Elmer Macrae, Walt Kuhn, and Henry Fitch Taylor. During one of the inevitable slow times during the exhibition, the four artists got together to lament difficulties in securing proper exhibits for innovative works within existing facilities. The idea came up that it might be a good idea for artists themselves to take charge of their own destinies by forming a society to promote and stage exhibitions that would create increased opportunities for all.

On December 14, 1911, the same four artists moved their discussions from the Madison Gallery to the studio of Jerome Myers, which was close by. In the first recorded minutes for the organization that became the Association of American Painters and Sculptors, Myers noted the objective "of organizing a society for the purpose of exhibiting works of progressive living painters—both American and foreign…" As a qualification, Myers added the intent of "favoring such work usually neglected by current shows and especially interesting and instructive to the public."

At the December 14 meeting, each of the four artists agreed to invite four others to participate as charter members at the next meeting of the new society. The next meeting was held on December 19 at the Madison Gallery. Henry Fitch Taylor served as host. Sixteen artists attended and four more expressed interest by proxy.

In an opening statement, Taylor set the tone of the new undertaking: it was to create an alternative to the National Academy as a showplace for current, living American art. Taylor expressed the specific feeling that the Academy did not represent the tastes of Americans and never did. A new forum was needed, he stressed.

Taylor was elected temporary president of the new organization and Kuhn became temporary secretary. The founding group accepted the provisional name of "American Painters and Sculptors." This was expanded shortly thereafter, when incorporation papers were filled out to read: "Association of American Artists and Sculptors."

The name of the new organization caused some later dissension among members. From the tone of the incorporation meeting, it was assumed that the Association would be dedicated to the showing of American art. The objectors had not been present at the original meeting of the four Madison Gallery exhibitors, which had adopted an objective of showing "both American and foreign" works. As members were added, some contention ensued.

As the scope of a proposed show took on broad international participation, some of the leaders of the art community of the day became uncomfortable. One such was Robert Henri. Henri was a charter member of the Association of American Painters and Sculptors and, initially, was slated to play an active organizational and leadership role. However, Henri was one of those committed to an American show. When it was clear that European artists would play major, possibly dominant, roles, he withdrew from Association leadership. However, he did exhibit in the group's Armory Show.

The move to internationalize the scope of the new Association's show was led by Davies and a group close to him. Though Davies had not been present at the December 14 meeting when the "American and foreign" resolution was adopted, he resurrected the original statement and strongly supported its intent.

At a January 2, 1912, meeting, a three-person committee was appointed to draft a constitution for presentation at the next meeting. The committee consisted of Arthur B. Davies, Gutzon Borglum, and John Mobray-Clarke. Borglum, a sculptor, initially proposed equal representation for painters and sculptors in offices and on committees. This was agreed to initially, but friction resulted before long because the painters far outnumbered sculptors and paintings figured far more prominently in exhibition plans.

As a guideline for constitutional drafters, Luks proposed and Myers seconded a motion that the principle of nonjury participation in shows be adopted. Officers were elected at the same January meeting. Provisionally, J. Alden Weir, who was not present then or at any subsequent meeting, was elected president. Borglum was named vice-president, Kuhn became secretary, and Macrae was elected treasurer.

In less than a year from the time of incorporation, the Association of American Painters and Sculptors, working on a shoestring with no aid from government, put together the massive event that changed the course of American art history.

Weir, who had not been present at the formation meetings or even during his provisional election, resigned the presidency. Some contemporaries attributed the resignation to a desire to avoid being in the forefront of the conflict that was evolving between the AAPS and the National Academy, of which Weir was a member. However, Weir did exhibit after his successors put together the massive Armory Show.

Arthur B. Davies was elected as the new president. Davies, of course, had a highly respectable position in American art as a member of The Eight. In addition, his extensive study in Europe gave him credentials to help promote the international flavor that members had determined the upcoming show should have. Until this time, Davies was seen as a retiring, mild-mannered (but competent) person. Once he took the reins at AAPS, however, he became a driving force, something of a tyrant capable of overwhelming obstacles that stood between him and success of his committed mission.

Davies traveled to Europe and enlisted participation from the leading modernists. He participated in negotiations for renting a larger exhibit facility than any that had previously been used for an artistic display. He helped raise contributions to underwrite a contract to rent the Sixty-Ninth Regiment Armory at Lexington Avenue and Twenty-fifth Street.

As the Armory Show's opening date of February 17, 1913, approached, paintings and sculpture pieces began to arrive by boat, train, and wagonload from Europe and the United States. In just a few days, the volunteer committees of the AAPS erected partitions in the barnlike Armory, then hung and mounted some 1,300 pieces of art. More than 80,000 people crowded into the exhibit during its one-month operation. After that, the same show, with only minor differences in the displayed pieces, traveled to the Art Institute of Chicago and Copley Hall in Boston.

As Henri had apparently feared—and as a number of his contemporaries had hoped—the European moderns dominated the public reaction to the Armory Show. Within a matter of months, American art acquired an entirely new dimension and demeanor. The social realism that had edged into prominence and public acceptance in 1908 at the expense of the rigidity of the National Academy now gave way itself to nonrepresentational and impressionist works. Names of artists who were barely known in America at the beginning of 1913 became bywords: Cezanne, Toulouse-Lautrec, Picasso, Matisse, Kandinsky, Monet, and Manet.

Modernism became dominant following the Armory Show. Alexander Kruse observed these developments. He watched some of his fellow artists and friends change their styles to climb onto the bandwagon of a seemingly irresistible trend. Kruse himself was not swayed. He developed an understanding for and a critical appreciation of the new trends. But he remained, as he grew intellectually closer to Sloan, Luks, and Henri, a "creative realist," a term he preferred as a description of his artistic philosophy. He was steadfast in maintaining this intellectual and artistic outlook even though he was out of step with the fads and trends that dominated the art world during much of his adult life.

Kruse's timing was also unfortunate in another respect: following in the example of his mentors, he had become an expert illustrator. He worked quickly, was able to produce excellent subject likenesses, and was masterful in his use of lines and tones. Had things continued the way they were, he might well have found a ready job market as a newspaper and magazine illustrator. However, at about the time Alex Kruse would have been ready to capitalize on his illustrating capabilities, the technology for image reproduction changed. Great improvements took place in the cameras and films that were available to photographers. In addition, photographic techniques were developed for the reproduction of photographs in newspapers. Demands for newspaper illustrators diminished quickly. Thus, despite his educational and professional progress, Alex Kruse still found himself having to develop other outlets so that he could earn a living.

Studies of Saxophone Player. (Drawing).

7
Adulthood

Following the thorough grounding Alex Kruse acquired through his work at the National Academy and Art Students League, he was awarded a credential as a full-time art teacher in 1909 by the New York Department of Education—a next-step-up from the summer-school credential awarded in 1906. In 1912, Kruse founded and directed his own art school, the Metropolis School of Art. He personally taught courses in drawing, still-life painting, and illustration. The school ran through 1913.

Later, he continued to teach in local schools while he was enrolled part-time in advanced composition, color, anatomy, and etching classes offered at the Art Students League. This study sequence began in 1916 and ran through 1921. From 1918 through 1920, Kruse worked under John Sloan in advanced studies of color composition. This experience helped cement the enduring relationship that Kruse maintained with Sloan. Sloan continued to be supportive and encouraging for his protege, as indicated in a comment noted in one of Kruse's diaries: "Sloan said: 'I can see by your work that you are a man that insists upon being yourself.'"

During the 1919-20 school year, Kruse studied etching with Mahonri

Alex Kruse as a young adult retained the closeness to his mother that endured throughout her life. This photo was taken about the time the family relocated to Harlem.

Young, who also became a friend, and also took classes in advanced anatomy drawing under George B. Bridgman. In the 1920-21 school year, Kruse returned to tutelage under Sloan and Luks. With Sloan, he studied life painting and pictorial composition. Luks was his instructor in portrait painting.

Kruse comments about his own work at that time in diary entries written during the 1960s:

How refreshingly it comes back to me, inspiringly I dare say, to recall what I felt about what I saw when a young artist had to look for side-lines to earn a livelihood and actually steal the time to go outdoors painting—or indoors.

Well-meaning relatives, friends and neighbors constantly offering unsolicited ideas on how to make a fast buck, the kind of painting that sells fast—without once questioning what was going on in my head and my mind. My mother was the tolerant one—my father always a bit skeptic. Yet these small early paintings accumulated and I hung on to them. Now there's one regret. Why didn't I produce more? Why did I use paint-remover on a good many just to save the piece of canvas?

I had to use small canvases purely for economy reasons. In some cases where cheaper colors were used, the paintings darkened, changed, and even faded—these I translated into lithographs and etchings in later years—the paintings weren't worth saving...

Nowadays I am no longer concerned with how to do it. That know-how I have at my finger-tips. Therefore, I am wholly concerned with what I am doing. Why should I be surprised that my painting looks better in a larger scale.

Although Robert Henri suggested my painting would look better if I painted on a larger scale, I felt then that I must wait till I feel [sic] ready craftwise to do that. It was only as I began to feel more and more that I want [sic] to project in my painting what I feel [sic] about what I see that I began to increase the size of my canvas. And yet, Mahonri Young said my earlier painting reminded him of the Little Dutch Masters, particularly Von Ostade. I went to the library to look up his work at that time and continued working within the 12x16/16x20 canvas size range for some years later.

During his years as an advanced student, Kruse maintained close contacts with a group of other advanced students who went on to illustrious careers on their own. These included Rockwell Kent, Peggy Bacon, Yasuo Kuniyoshi, William Zorach, Alexander Brook, Reginald Marsh, and Lena Gurr.

Years later, Alex Kruse was fond of telling an anecdote about the close, almost communal relationship that existed among members of the group consisting of Henri, Sloan, and their friends and followers. There was a company over in New Jersey that made artist's colors. (Like a true New York native, Kruse spoke the words "New Jersey" as a synonym for "foreign.") This paint manufacturer had the misfortune to sell a single tube of cobalt blue paint that was used by John Sloan. After about two years, the paint turned black right on the canvas. The following year, the New Jersey house was out of business; such were the communication links in the art community in those days.

By this time, Kruse's illustration skills were considerable. With opportunities limited in news departments of newspapers, he turned to the fields of fashion and advertising. Starting in 1917, he worked as an illustrator for one year with the Osgood Studios, maintaining a 48-hour-per-week work schedule while still finding time to keep up with Art Students League classes and completing his school assignments. This pace continued through 1922. After leaving the Osgood Studios, Kruse was employed full time at the L. A. Westerman Company, which had offices in the Flatiron Building at Fifth Avenue and Twenty-third Street. Later, he worked part time for two separate studios in the East Village area of Lower Manhattan: Wright Illustration Company and F. C. Stevens Company, a large retailer.

During this era, Kruse continued a habit started back in his Educational Alliance days; he carried a sketch pad with him everywhere and recorded encountered images incessantly. With experience. he increased both productivity and sophistication of his rough sketches. He would rough out a pencil sketch of either a complete scene or a pictorial element that appealed to him, such as a tree or a workman in a pose that would fit into an in-work composition. He would then write in notes about colors or special features of his subject matter, sometimes through marginal notes with arrows leading to applicable portions of his sketch and sometimes with notations right in the image areas themselves.

Kruse's purpose was to capture first impressions of compositions that held potential for him. In effect, he created a warehouse—perhaps a better simile would be that he was creating deposits for an idea bank, with each new sketch adding anew to his positive balance. Literally, he made withdrawals from this bank of ideas throughout his life for prints and paintings that could be developed in accordance with his activity pattern at any given time. To dramatize this trait, the last painting he completed before his death at eighty-four was created from a sketch he drew in the fall of 1923, on his honeymoon. He left literally a trunk full of sketch pads and drawings on loose sheets of paper, an idea bank that could easily have provided inspiration sources for another eighty-four years.

At 82, he wrote in his diary:

> I have many canvases started. When an idea strikes, I make an immediate record of it graphically. I use any medium that happens to be handy, pencil, or charcoal, or pastel. When the compulsion to express myself grips, I proceed at once to make a note of it while I'm thinking about it. Over the years I have accumulated a wealth of paintable ideas. Some compositions have lent themselves better on the lithograph stone or perhaps copper etching or drypoint or some other phase of etching or pastel. The overall idea is that when I get up in the morning, I don't have to look for something to do.
>
> So that when someone asks me where is your latest work? My answer is it may be any one of those canvases (especially) which I have completed recently if I don't have a date on it. I allow no painting to leave my studio-workshop until I feel I have accomplished what I felt about what I saw during my first impression.
>
> What I enjoy most is painting variations on a theme—a theme over which I have already gone through the pleasant labor-pains of re-creational pictorial composition.

In 1922, Alex Kruse met and formed a close-fitting match with Anna Wecht. On the surface, this was an unlikely courtship, particularly for the time period involved. Anna was fourteen years younger than Alex, a spread that drew disapproval from her family. The geography of their courtship was also unlikely. The Kruses lived in Harlem, a world apart from the Williamsburg section of Brooklyn where the Wechts made their home. Anna's father and mother ran a dairy market. (Under Jewish dietary laws, food stores can sell meat or dairy products, never a mixture if they are to be considered Kosher.) Anna and her brother Harold, two years younger, helped out in the business.

The Kruses were a small nuclear family consisting of father, mother, and one child. Lena and Sigmund each had one sibling. The Wechts, who emigrated to the United States from Riga, capital of Latvia, were a family of three brothers and a sister. Jenny Charles, Anna's mother, came from a family that included two sisters and three brothers, all living in relatively close proximity to one another.

The Wecht and Charles families included an accountant, an attorney, and an assortment of small businesspeople, providing no background in nor exposure to the arts for Anna. But the interests developed anyway. Anna had an excellent singing voice and, largely on her own, studied piano and became a proficient accompanist. Later, she developed into a hostess of note, building on traits that her mother described as being "a natural mixer." From her mother, who was the driving force in running the family business, Anna also acquired large measures of ambition and diligence, as well as a storekeeper's natural skill with numbers and an eye for details. She had the attributes necessary to become a lifetime partner and pillar of strength to help Alex gain the time and build the confidence to pursue his artistic opportunities. When Alexander Kruse became a critic and author, Anna Kruse was there as a highly competent editor and manuscript typist. (Alex never did learn to use a typewriter.) She also developed earning capacity

Industrial Pagodas. (Lithograph). Proximity to Coney Island led Kruse to produce this kind of cityscape.

which enabled her to provide for much—during some lean years, most—of the income needed to sustain the family.

Surmounting real and imaginary obstacles related to their age difference, courtship travel distance, and the reservations about marrying an artist with no regular weekly income, Anna Wecht and Alexander Kruse were married on October 31, 1923. Their honeymoon arrangements fit their budget limitations: they spent their honeymoon on a farm in Robinsville, New Jersey, where the owners took in boarders. Alex sketched; Anna provided admiration and support, as she was to do for forty-eight years. One of the honeymoon sketches, showing the barnyard area of the farm, was the source for Alex Kruse's final painting in 1972.

Following the wedding, the Kruses set up housekeeping in an area of Brooklyn that was equivalent to what later became known as suburbia. Farmers were still raising and marketing vegetables across the street and on the next block. But the farms were giving way rapidly to semi-attached, single-family dwellings that gave families like the Kruses an opportunity to live and raise their families in homes of their own. The area where the Kruses lived for the next twenty years was called Mapleton Park by some residents. For others, it was part of the larger Brooklyn neighborhood known as Bensonhurst. The Kruse home was at 1753 Sixty-fourth Street.

As the area was laid out, this meant the house was midway between Seventeenth and Eighteenth Avenues. Development of the area where the Kruses purchased their home resulted from completion of a series of four subway lines that ran between Times Square in midtown Manhattan and Coney Island, a beach resort at the southern tip of Brooklyn. The Kruse home was on the Sea Beach Line, with the Eighteenth Avenue station around the corner.

Eighteenth Avenue was one of the main commercial thoroughfares of Bensonhurst, settled by a mixture that consisted chiefly of Jewish families migrating from Harlem and Italians who came from the Lower East Side, The Bronx, or "Italian Harlem." The intensity of the ethnic mix was demonstrated for the family some years later when two neighborhood boys who had been playing on the street came running into one boy's home to ask the father to resolve an argument. The son asked: "Is President Roosevelt Jewish or Italian?" These ethnic choices represented the totality of the children's ancestral awareness.

Alex's parents, Lena and Sigmund, moved into the Brooklyn home with the newlywed couple, a typical retirement arrangement for aging parents in those days. The building was modified to enclose an open front porch for use as a studio by Alex. By then, Alex was concentrating his artistic efforts in the field of printmaking, though he worked in oil continuously—then and for the remainder of his life. Through the late twenties and thirties, the Weyhe Gallery handled Kruse prints. Carl Zigrosser, an authority and recognized historian on printmaking, became Alex Kruse's friend and dealer. During these years, Zigrosser served as Weyhe's gallery director. The gallery had special portfolios printed for presentations of Kruse's prints.

Under Anna's ministrations, the Kruse home became a hospitality center for artistic and literary friends, as well as for the many family members and personal friends who still lived in the distant lands across the East River—in Manhattan, The Bronx, or even New Jersey. On many late nights, Anna would play the piano while guests, an occasional professional musician among them, would sing the popular songs of the day.

At about this time, with sympathy on the left running high for the social experiments in Russia, *The New Masses* was born as an attempt to revive the spirit and zeal of the "old" *Masses*. Alex Kruse, always amenable to suggestions and guidance from John Sloan, signed on as art director, providing frequent illustrations and soliciting contributed illustrations from his old socialist friends. Among the editors of *The New Masses* was Stanley Burnshaw, who became a close personal friend and who encouraged the Kruses in their later literary efforts. Stanley Burnshaw was a poet, biographer, and editor who went on to enjoy great success and wealth as a publisher of college textbooks. He and a number of literary and artistic friends were frequent guests during evening get-togethers at the Kruse home. John Sloan was a frequent visitor, as were Peggy Bacon, Jerome and Ethel Myers, and others of the circle that had built up around the Art Students League and *The Masses.*

On the other side of the political spectrum, Alex and Anna Kruse maintained a subway-commuting closeness to the Medalie family, particularly George and his wife, Carrie. By this time, the Medalie family had set itself up in a ten-room luxury apartment in one of the most prestigious buildings on Manhattan's West Side, the Belnord, located at Broadway and Eighty-sixth Street. George Medalie had become one of the most successful corporate attorneys in the country, a leading Republican who would run for United States Senate during the Republican debacle of 1932 which swept Franklin D. Roosevelt into office. During the twenties, George Medalie was impressed by a young law student whom he hired as a law clerk in his firm. This protege, Thomas E. Dewey, went on to become governor of New York and a two-time Republican presidential candidate. Had Dewey been elected in 1944, George Medalie would almost certainly have become Attorney General.

As Medalie kept enhancing his circle of acquaintances and his influence, his friendship proved peripherally beneficial to Alex Kruse's ability to maintain himself financially and to enhance his reputation, particularly through the tribulations of the Great Depression, which imposed hardships in meeting mortgage payments on the home purchased during the easygoing twenties. George and Carrie Medalie, through the years, purchased scores of prints from their cousin for use as gifts to influential friends. A number of portrait commissions, including one of George himself, also derived from Medalie's kinship and loyalty.

The Brooklyn roots, which sprouted quickly and deeply, helped add to Alex Kruse's commitment to America as a source of artistic direction and inspiration. The period during which the Kruses settled in Brooklyn was a heyday of expatriate activity in Paris. Many acquaintances paid visits of homage and participation to the clique that included Gertrude Stein, Ernest Hemingway, Isadora Duncan, and F. Scott Fitzgerald, as well as Davies and Prendergast. Kruse insisted throughout his life that he could find all the inspiration and subject matter he needed in the United States.

From the time of their marriage, Anna and Alex Kruse had a tacit understanding that, if their firstborn child was a boy, they would name him John Sloan Kruse. The intent represents a good measure of the esteem in which Alex held his close friend and mentor. As human plans went, this seemed like a sure thing, provided, of course, that the Kruses had a son.

Jewish tradition prohibits naming a child after a living relative. Since Anna's father, Benjamin Wecht, was only forty-nine when she became pregnant in 1925, the prospects were good for Sloan to acquire a namesake—if the child turned out to be a boy.

Fate intervened. At the Passover Sedar (festival dinner) in April, 1925, Benjamin Wecht dropped dead in the Kruse's home. When the boy was born on December 13, 1925, he was named Benjamin at first. A few weeks later, at the urging of Alex's cousin, Carmina Medalie, the Kruse's agreed to change their son's name to Benedict.

But John Sloan knew of the original intent. Since he was childless himself, the intent made a major impression. Sloan showed an uncle-like interest in the boy during his early years. In 1928, Sloan inscribed a memento to his honorary nephew. Sloan had created the official poster for the Artists' and Models' Ball that fall. He attached the linoleum cut from which the poster was printed to a proof of the finished piece, which he autographed to "Benedict John Sloan Kruse."

The relationship and attendant interest in the boy continued. At a party for Ben's fifth birthday in 1930, Sloan and most of the "Masses crowd" were among the celebrants. Mementos of that party are still in the family. One of the guests was Wanda G'ag, the creative, innovative author/illustrator of children's books, including the classic *Millions of Cats*. This book and a subsequent volume, *The Funny Thing,* were published in 1929 by Coward McCann, Inc., from original woodcuts by the author. Autographed copies of these books have remained in the family through the years, having been put to good use as they were read to three Kruse grandchildren.

The following Spring, a doting Alex Kruse set up a paintbox, brushes, and canvas and presented them to his son with great expectations. In one attempt at painting, Ben made a mess of the canvas and Alex gave up. It turned out just as well. Rather than drawing and painting together, Alex and his son devoted many afternoons to tossing a baseball or football back and forth in the driveway alongside their home. In the long run, Alex Kruse gained more than a son; he acquired a model for a number of portraits and figure paintings developed over the course of the remainder of his lifetime.

As one result of having a son he was close to, Alex Kruse saw a lot of Coney Island while Ben was growing up. In those days, Coney Island was an extremely popular resort and leisure center that boasted two major amusement parks and a long, white, sandy beach fronted by an ocean still clean enough for swimming. Coney Island was a favorite place for Brooklynites to swim, picnic, and generally escape from oppressive summer heat. For Alex and Ben, Coney Island was ten to fifteen minutes away on the subway, perhaps an hour if they walked. They frequently walked there, with multiple pauses for Alex to sketch scenes or people who caught his eye, then rode back. A substantial body of work—including drawings, prints, and paintings, evolved from these father-son excursions.

Motordome, Coney Island. (Oil, 16 1/4" x 12 1/4"). With the move to Brooklyn, Coney Island became a place for summer escape and a destination for long walks by Alex and Ben Kruse.

On A Break. (Drawing).

Inspection. (Drawing).

8
Building Professional Stature

The house in Brooklyn provided enough working and storage space to permit Alex Kruse finally to accumulate and store a substantial body of work. During the years following his marriage, he established himself as a first-rank professional in two separate media: printmaking and painting.

He also embarked on an ambitious program of submitting work to and exhibiting in major shows, often with paintings and prints hanging side by side. Unfortunately, some of the records of shows, lectures, and writings were lost in various moves from Brooklyn to Manhattan and then to Los Angeles twice with a return to New York in between. However, publications and documents that survived are sufficient to provide a basis for recounting some of Alex's major exhibition activities, as summarized below.

During earlier political and professional activities, Kruse participated in a wide range of activities of the Independent Artists of America and the Salons of America. The Independents, founded in 1910 by members of The American Eight, sponsored nonjuried shows open to artists who followed any school or style of painting, drawing, or sculpture. The group remained active through the 1920s and 1930s. Many established artists took part in these showings and enjoyed brisk sales of their works. The Independents' shows also provided an entry threshold for many novice artists.

The Salons of America had a more conservative leaning that favored representational works. Salon shows also were nonjuried. This organization remained active for a number of years. After his marriage, Kruse stepped up his participation in the Salons as well as with the Independents.

Another activity in which Kruse was active during the 1920s involved attempts to form a union of artists. Alex's friend and former fellow student, Rockwell Kent, was one of the leaders of this effort. The union never materialized. But the attempts kept Alex in touch with and active in political causes for a number of years.

In particular, Kruse was incensed over the treatment of Sacco and Vanzetti, the Italian immigrants and active anarchists who were executed for a murder which, according to their supporters, they did not commit and could not have committed because they were nowhere near the scene. Nicola Sacco and Bartolomeo Vanzetti were accused of committing a holdup at a Boston-area shoe factory in 1921. In the course of the holdup, a paymaster was murdered. Trials and appeals dragged on for six years. Finally, they were executed by electrocution on August 23, 1927.

At the time, Kruse was connected with *The New Masses,* which took a strong stand in support of Sacco and Vanzetti. Alex Kruse reacted with a large painting (the largest in the family collection on his death) called *A Boston Sunset.* The background of the painting shows a seashore at sunset. In the foreground are two large wooden crosses on which the anarchists are being crucified by capitalists in tuxedos and top hats. During the late 1920s and into the early 1930s, the painting was shown, to striking effect, at a show of the Independents and other exhibitions of liberal organizations.

Alex Kruse participated in a group show that opened in the prestigious Dudensing Galleries in Manhattan on May 10, 1924. The show was reviewed by critics from the *New York Sun* and the *Brooklyn Eagle.* (Though it was a local paper with circulation chiefly in the borough of Brooklyn, the *Eagle* had considerable prestige, partly because of the large population of Brooklyn, which would have been the nation's fourth largest city if it had been independent, and partly because the paper enjoyed a rich heritage that dated back to its founding by Walt Whitman.)

In reviewing the Dudensing show, the critic for the *Sun* cited works by Kruse and Louis Eilshemius and observed: "In choosing the pictures for this show, the qualities that have appealed most to Mr. Dudensing, apparently, have been freshness of viewpoint and freedom from self-consciousness." The *Eagle* reviewer noted that "George Constant, Fred Gardner, Alexander Kruse, and Ernest Stock are more in the light of discoveries."

Kruse's personal notes indicate that, as happened frequently during this period, all of the pictures he exhibited were sold.

By this time, Kruse was committed to a plan of work that saw him producing between three and five etchings or lithographs each year. During this period, printmaking prospered as part of a longstanding continuum under which the medium was respected in the New York art world as a highly skilled specialty, carrying on traditions that continued until the early 1940s. The potential problem in printmaking is that the artist does not control the appearance of the finished product as happens with a painting. The end product of the printmaking art is an impression taken from a copper plate or heavy, smooth-surfaced stone. The quality of the work that hangs on the wall depends largely on the skill of the printmaker. Thus, the value ascribed to the print could depend on the credentials and skill of the craftsman who did the printing.

To assure quality, the process of pulling prints from a plate or stone usually requires a collaborative effort between artist and printer. Alex Kruse insisted on being present when prints were pulled for him. The process inevitably included discussions about desired values, application of inks, and review of proofs and final prints.

The people with whom Kruse collaborated in producing prints were highly respected professionals, each at the top of his respective craft. Lithographs were printed by George Miller, a respected authority and author of a number of books on printmaking. Etchings were printed in the studio of Frank Nankivell, an accomplished etcher himself and participant in the Armory Show and other major exhibitions. Nankivell also wrote extensively on etching technique in art journals. These experts provided an infrastructure that helped Kruse build recognition as one of the country's top printmakers during the period that started early in the 1920s and extended to the early 1940s.

During the early 1940s, unfortunately, printmaking was virtually destroyed as an economically viable artistic medium. In 1941, an organization called Associated American Artists was formed. The promoters of the AAA purchased, outright, a number of plates and stones from popular artists, then ran unlimited editions of relatively few works. Over a period of hundreds of years, dating back to Rembrandt's time, prints had been produced in limited editions. The value of prints was derived partly from the fact that supplies were limited. That changed when Associated American Artists came on the scene. AAA marketing was done through mass mailings of illustrated brochures. All prints were sold at $5 per copy, a fraction of the price set on prints made under traditional controls and quality standards. In the face of such competition, legitimate galleries could no longer afford to carry and sell prints. Professional artists could not earn a livelihood from printmaking.

After centuries of tradition and continuity of artistic effort, the market for prints was drastically diminished. Starting in the 1940s, Kruse concentrated almost completely on painting as his preferred medium. However, as indicated, the decades beginning with the 1920s represented a printmaker's heyday. Accordingly, many of the citations that follow deal with showings of Kruse prints.

In March, 1926, Kruse participated in the Eleventh Annual Exhibition of the Whitney Studio Club, which included painting and sculpture and was hosted at the Anderson Galleries, Park Avenue and Fifty-seventh Street. Kruse showed a lithograph entitled *Third Avenue,* a scene showing tired passengers inside an el train.

On the Ferryboat. (Lithograph.).

In September of the same year, several Kruse prints were included in a group show at the Weyhe Gallery. A review in the *New York Sun* discussed the exhibited lithographs in detail, highlighting works by George Biddle, Alexander Kruse, and Reginald Marsh. The reviewer commented: "Three lithographs by the New York artist, A.Z. Cruse [sic], display power and a facility in the handling of weighty forms."

A month later, the Opportunity Gallery featured lithographs by A.Z. Kruse and Boardman Robinson. The two titles by Kruse were *In East Harlem* and *On the Ferryboat.* The first shows jazz musicians in Harlem's Cotton Club. The second shows workers loading a horsedrawn wagon as they prepare to remove cargo from the boat.

A feature article about Kruse's commitment to America in his art resulted from his participation in a group show at the Weyhe Gallery in November, 1929. The article, by art critic Ben Slater, appeared in a magazine, the *Jewish Tribune.* The headline carried the title: "Alexander Z. Kruse—An American-Made Artist." Slater stressed Kruse's commitment to training and working in America at a time when, at least according to the writer, the majority of noteworthy American artists had felt it necessary to go to Europe for their inspiration and training.

Slater's interview with Kruse also dealt with Alex's rebellion against the limitations of academic art. Kruse was quoted as saying he wasn't sure just when his sense of frustration with the inflexibility of literal realism set in. However, the article noted that Kruse had some distinct ideas on "creative realism." Kruse was quoted as follows: "An artist's work should register his thoughts and his particular sensitiveness. Too many artists, lacking in imagination, strive after a literal translation of what the eye beholds and, as a result, their work is merely photographic. Or else they are imitative, content to submerge their own individuality in that of another."

Here Comes the Bride. (Woodcut).

The article admired Kruse's ability to find inspiration in painting or sketching subjects of urban life. Commenting on the nonobjective trends of the day, Kruse told Slater he did not believe "in creating aesthetic puzzles." The critic concluded that he felt Kruse's work had enough form and perspective to keep academic critics at bay.

Although the country was beginning to sink into the Great Depression in 1930, that year was crowded with exhibition activities for Alex Kruse. He received a letter in January advising him that two of his lithographs, *In East Harlem* and *The German Band,* had been accepted for showing in the First International Exhibition of Lithography and Wood Engraving, to be held in the Art Institute of Chicago beginning that same month. In covering the event, *The New York Times* included a photograph of Kruse, along with a descriptive caption, in its rotogravure section.

Also in January, Kruse, his former classmate Reginald Marsh, and other artists were included in an exhibition of lithographs and paintings at the Weyhe Gallery.

In March of the same year, three Kruse lithographs were hung in the annual exhibition of the Society of Independent Artists, held in the mammoth Grand Central Palace. The pieces shown were *The German Band, The Window Cleaners,* and *Back From the Country.*

Also in March, the American Institute of Graphic Arts opened a traveling exhibition entitled Fifty Prints of the Year. The works in the show, selected by John Sloan, included a Kruse lithograph entitled *Musical Clown.*

In April, the Salons of America held its annual show. A Kruse woodcut entitled *Here Comes the Bride* was included.

All of these spring, 1930, activities merited coverage by New York's major newspapers, which reproduced several Kruse works.

To round out Alex Kruse's busy 1930, December brought a number of noteworthy events:

The Fourth Annual Exhibition of the American Print Makers was held in the Downtown Gallery. Four Kruse prints were shown: *A Distinguished Audience, City Hall, Spuyten Duyvil,* and *East Side,* which was reproduced in the exhibition catalog.

During the same month, the Second International Exhibition of Lithography and Wood Engravings opened at the Art Institute of Chicago. This show continued into the following January. Kruse's *The Musical Clown* was reproduced in the catalog.

Finally, a portfolio collection of Kruse lithographs assembled by Carl Zigrosser for the Weyhe Gallery was reviewed at the end of the year by E. C. Sherburne, art critic for the *Christian Science Monitor.* This article included analysis of salient compositional, stylistic, and technical features of Kruse's work. Using *Spuyten Duyvil No. 1* as a primary example, Sherburne pointed out the solidity of form, integrity of volumes, and symmetry of foliage in the rendition of trees, a frequently cited strength in Kruse's work. The critic found a balance of contrasts between straight lines and curves in the topographic layout of the scene that included a small inlet with a boat landing. Kruse's compositional balance could withstand the test if the print was turned upside down; that is, the values of light and dark forms remain sound from any perspective. This comment reflects a recognition of Kruse's idea of creative realism, a belief that it is up to the artist to arrange elements taken from nature rather than simply recording the literal image presented to the eye.

Sherburne praised Kruse's well executed tonal transitions and his sensitivity for "accents and variation within repetition," which were seen as strengthening the overall composition of the work. The critic also liked the overall sculptural emphasis and fascinating texture obtained by "impeded movement of the crayon."

Sherburne also commented on a strong consciousness of the times that was apparent in Kruse's depiction of musical performers on stage, in cafe life, or in street bands, while his social satire involved diverse combinations of human figures in urban life.

Along with virtually everyone else in the art world, Alex Kruse suffered a profound sense of loss with the passing of his teacher, Robert Henri, in 1929 at the comparatively young age of 64. Kruse considered it an important recognition of Henri's contributions when The Metropolitan Museum of Art held a commemorative exhibition of Henri's paintings in March, 1931. John Sloan helped to select the works that were shown and also wrote the foreword for the exhibition catalog, a copy of which Kruse kept throughout his life.

Back from the Country. (Lithograph.).

Also during March, 1931, the Society of Independent Artists opened its annual exhibition at the Grand Central Palace. E.C. Sherburne, who reviewed both shows for *The Christian Science Monitor,* faulted the Independents for showing many works that he considered to be "crude, inept, tasteless or violent." Sherburne added that "the artist must not only have something to say, but must know how to say it." Then the critic noted that he also encountered "accomplished pictures and sculptures, only to find that they are by artists already well known, such as Alexander Z. Kruse, Fredrick Detwiller, David Burliuk, Walter Pach, A. Walkowitz, and others."

One of Kruse's works included in the Independents' show, *Back From the Country,* a humorous piece showing a well dressed woman weighing herself on a large scale, was reproduced both in *The New York Evening Post* and the *Chicago Evening Post.*

A *New York Times* review of a comprehensive show encompassing multiple artistic styles at the Weyhe Gallery in August, 1931, identified paintings by Siqueiros, Georgia O'Keefe, Alexander Z. Kruse, Alfred Maurer, as well as drawings by Degas and Cezanne and lithographs by Rockwell Kent. This was the first time that Kruse had included paintings at a major Weyhe show. One of his paintings, *Portrait of a Doll,* was reproduced in the *Chicago Evening Post.* The painting positions a Shirley Temple doll prominently in the foreground before a background similar in technique and style to Kruse's renditions of the Spuyten Duyvil scene. The painting had been commissioned by Ideal Toy Company, which manufactured and sold millions of the dolls in the Shirley Temple likeness.

Kruse figured in a major article by Carl Zigrosser that appeared in the November, 1931, issue of *Creative Art* magazine under the title "Modern American Graphic Art" (pp. 369-74). Zigrosser noted an emphasis on American themes and what he saw as a creative thrust that depicted urban existence in terms of its human ramifications. In the area of etching, he cited the work of John Sloan, Edward Hopper, Kenneth Hays Miller, Peggy Bacon, and Reginald Marsh as pioneers.

In lithography, Zigrosser cited Alexander Kruse for his intensely personal style and included Mabel Dwight and Glenn Coleman as potent contributors to the "observation and documentation of life in the urban scene of New York City and its humorous side."

Zigrosser included Kruse in a group of innovative artists for whom he predicted a crucial role in American graphic art because he felt their treatment of the importance and beauty of American urban life was destined to contribute to an emerging national consciousness. Others in the group included Rockwell Kent, Hopper, Kuniyoshi, Louis Lozowick, John Marin, and Marsh.

In addition to concentrating on his own production and maintaining a hectic exhibition schedule, Kruse also continued to teach. In November, 1931, he took over direction of a series of Saturday and evening classes at the New York School of Design, located at 625 Madison Avenue. Courses included portraiture and figure drawing. On Thursday evenings, Kruse moderated an open-forum discussion aimed at stimulating art appreciation.

At about this time, Kruse launched a career as a lecturer on art, artists, and art history. Demand for his appearances grew through the years as he demonstrated a capability for making art relevant and interesting for lay people. Using resources such as the vast collection of slides available through the Metropolitan Museum, he was able to tailor his presentations to the interests of individual groups or to build a sequence of lectures to initiate listeners into an understanding of the history and evolution of art from early times to current trends.

Kruse's skill as a lecturer was noted in an article in the *Staten Island Advance* in January, 1932, by George Kennedy, which covered a slide lecture on modern art at the Jewish Community Center in Tompkinsville. The article comments particularly on the eloquence with which Kruse praised his teacher, John Sloan, and on his clarity in describing the role of art as a reflection of both the ugliness and beauty in modern life.

An important new level of recognition was achieved in 1932, when a number of Kruse prints were acquired for two highly prestigious, permanent collections. The Metropolitan Museum of Art acquired six Kruse lithographs for its permanent print collection. One of these was a lithographic self-portrait. In addition, the New York Public Library, a noted collector of fine prints, acquired a number of lithographs.

Concurrently, Kruse's exhibition schedule continued unabated. During the early part of 1932, his works were included in shows at the Carnegie Institute Art Gallery, Pittsburgh, the Art Institute of Chicago, the Grand Central Art Gallery, and the Weyhe Gallery.

In April, 1932, in connection with the inclusion of several Kruse lithographs in a show at the Delphic Gallery that also featured George Bellows' *Stag at Sharkey's,* Kruse spoke on some of his ideas on artistic creativity to a reporter from the *New York Evening Journal.* The article quoted Kruse as saying: "A poet that has been swept away by a dream or a musician that might be contemplating a symphony does not know what will result. So with a painter. He takes a brush and is guided by his mind. Time is nothing, everything is nothing to the artist until he has spent himself." When the reporter, noting the hard times of the Great Depression, asked about ways to fight discouragement in artistic endeavors, Kruse replied: "For others I do not know, but for me the subject is stronger than I am. I go away, come back, leave but always return. I cannot help myself."

Rivera Speaks. (Pastel, 24" x 30").

The Delphic Gallery show was also reviewed by Edward Alden Jewell for *The New York Times.* Jewell commented that he found Kruse's *Young Smoker* to be "The most convincing of A. Z. Kruse's prints the writer has yet seen."

At the tenth exhibition of the Salons of America, which ran concurrently with the Delphic Gallery show but ended a few weeks later (in May, 1932), Kruse offered the first public view of his sympathetic pastel portrait, *Diego Rivera Speaks.* In her review of the show, Margaret Breuning called the portrait "a lively presentment of the vigorous artist in action haranguing the beholder with vehemence." Breuning also commented on what she felt to be a significant upgrading of the improved quality of the works shown in this no-prize, no-jury show.

An unsigned review in the *Christian Science Monitor* praised the Rivera portrait this way: "Mr. A.Z. Kruse, in a canvas utilizing both pastel and paint, conveys a jolly report of *Rivera Speaks* that is at once good in characterization and handsome in color."

Kruse received even more favorable responses at the exhibition entitled "Portraits of Artists" held at the Roerich Museum in New York in November, 1932. The review in the *New York Sun* found the show full of "Extraordinary types in a selection of over sixty entries. The portraits ranged all the way from Fantin-Latour and James Caroll Beckwith's Carolus Duran to Charles W. Hawthorne, Foujita, Max Bohm, and Haley Lever." The reporter made a special note of Kruse's *Rivera Speaks* and Andre Derain's portrait of Kisling.

In a separate review of the portrait show, Buell Hueston, writing in *The Greenwich Villager,* admired Kruse's portrait of Diego Rivera, very much of a local hero in the Village since his mural, originally destined for Rockefeller Center, was to be installed in the Memorial Library of the Rand School and was to be put on exhibit in the Village Tea Room, a restaurant in the Village that had been set up in a renovated barn. (During the days of horsedrawn carriages, many New York homes had their own stables and many neighborhoods had barns that boarded horses. Many stables were later remodeled into small theaters or restaurants.)

Recognition of Kruse and the stature he had acquired in painting, lithography, and etching came in an article in the June, 1933, issue of the *Spectator* magazine by Dagney Edwards. In part, the article included a serious review of Kruse's motivational and artistic development.

Citing what he felt to be profundity and symbolism of Kruse's imagery, Edwards explained that the artist "adhered strictly to his principle, becoming with his brush the symbolical interpreter of the character and emotions of the common everyday individuals known to us all." Edwards concluded: "Mr. Kruse creates, without models, human interest subjects that are, in the words of Frank Crowninshield, editor of *Vanity Fair* magazine 'Forthright and Moving!' They are not only alive with feeling and expressions, but contain such depth that their ultimate motive, their TRUE interpretation, must depend wholly upon the beholder's psychological and philosophical sense of values." Kruse's success was also related to his wide range of dramatic subjects drawn from human life.

The *Spectator* article by Edwards also lauded Kruse's commitment to America for his inspiration and subject matter. Edwards noted that Kruse refused to study abroad. Then Kruse was quoted: "I'm not one of those artists who ever felt the necessity for going abroad to study…From my personal observation during the past decade, American artists return with the spectacles of some foreign success of the moment."

In an unsigned *New York Times* review of the exhibition of The One Hundred Best Prints of the Year of American and European Artists in 1933, Kruse's name was singled out for mention along with his friends and colleagues Peggy Bacon, Childe Hassam, and Mahonri Young. The show, held at the Brooklyn Museum, opened on December 12, 1934. In the catalog for the exhibition, Susan Hutchinson, the show's curator, acknowledged Kruse's status as a Brooklyn artist, then praised his work, noting that he was "a lithographer as well as an etcher and his *Long Island Peasant* [on exhibit], a combination of etching and aquatint, may show the influence of the crayon, but withall it is an individualistic expression of landscape in which form is the prevailing feature."

George Luks in Action. (Oil, 30" x 30").

In a review of the same show, *New York Times* critic Elizabeth Luther Cary admired Kruse's compositional and technical dexterity visible in the *Long Island Peasant,* stating: "The finely marshaled rhythms of the grassy dunes are what makes the activity of the picture, into which we deeply plunge toward the calm of smooth water. The medium is aquatint combined with etching and the combination under Mr. Kruse's knowing management makes for stimulus and liveliness."

Toward the end of 1933, Kruse's practice of developing paintings from memo-type sketches served him well. After George Luks died in October, 1933, Kruse started work almost immediately to convert sketches from Luks's class at the Art Students League into a painting entitled *George Luks in Action.* The painting shows Luks, wearing a cowboy hat, busily at work on a painting of a model posing as a dancer. The painting was featured in the next exhibition in which Kruse participated, a show for the work of Brooklyn and Long Island artists at the Brooklyn Museum that ran from the end of January through February 26, 1934. A total of more than 100 artists were represented, including Max Weber, Maurice Sterne, Abraham Walkowitz, Agden Pleissner, and several painters who had moved directly to Brooklyn on emigrating from Europe.

In addition to the Luks piece, Kruse submitted seven other paintings. R.C. Sherburne, in his review for the *Christian Science Monitor* wrote: "Mr. Kruse shows, in a group of eight paintings, how design and color vision can build upon actuality…In *George Luks in Action,* the comment is at once truthful and humorous. *Portrait of My Mother* is persuasive in its unforced verity, and *Young Troubadour* indicates the artist's discovery of beauty in the common life as it is."

Howard Devree of *The New York Times* also noted the presence of Kruse's *George Luks in Action.*

In addition to this immediate reaction to the shock of the loss of a close friend, Kruse was motivated to write a commemorative article about Luks, which appeared in the February, 1934, issue of the *Greenwich Villager* magazine. This article, in turn, helped launch Kruse as a writer of note, particularly as a critic and commentator about art. The chapter that follows digresses to discuss and present some relevant examples of Kruse's early success with his writing.

The Ford's End

9
'Art to Heart Talks'

By the beginning of 1934, Alexander Kruse had already established that he was skilled in expressing himself in words as well as with paint, charcoal, and litho crayons. He also had established himself as a promising teacher and lecturer, enjoying increasing demand for his services in these areas.

An event that took place on October 29, 1933, moved Alex Kruse to a new level in his use of words and helped to establish him as a recognized writer on art. As noted in the previous chapter, the event, not unexpected, was the death of George Luks in a barroom brawl. Luks had been fading for some time previously; the fact that he had lived for sixty-seven years was seen by some as a tribute to the preservative power of alcohol.

As Alex Kruse thought back on the memories evoked by Luks's passing, he literally was moved to pick up a pencil. That's the way he wrote throughout the remainder of his life. Alex drafted by longhand; Anna typed—and touched up the spelling and grammar as she went.

The first major Kruse work in print was an article that ran in the February, 1934, issue of *The Greenwich Villager* magazine under the title

"Luks Still Lives in His Work, Wit and Wisdom." The article was devoted mostly to a serious review of Luks's philosophy as an artist and techniques as a teacher. Kruse himself had come to believe devoutly in instruction through demonstration. He also respected and emulated Luks in terms of the older man's commitment to draftsmanship as a foundation for artistic creativity. Beyond that, Luks was hailed as a practical human being who showed great resourcefulness in being able to support himself through whatever means necessary—from prizefighting to professional entertainment to commercial illustration—so that he could practice his art creatively. Kruse also believed firmly, with Luks, that creative art was one part of the painter's life that should not be for sale, should not be prostituted at any price.

The *Villager* article also recounted an incident that demonstrated Luks's quickness with an ever-present sense of humor. This incident was reprinted in the first of a series of short vignettes that Kruse offered to his friend, Peyton Boswell, Sr., then editor of the *Art Digest*. Kruse chose the title *Art to Heart Talks*. The first, which appeared on April 15, 1934, reprinted the Luks anecdote referred to above. After that, additional *Art to Heart Talks* ran periodically and sporadically for the next seven years. In total, these pieces present an insight into Kruse's personality and philosophy. Accordingly, the surviving collection of these chats is reprinted on the pages that follow in the belief that the reader will find them both amusing and informative.

April 15, 1934
How Luks Explained It

On one occasion, when Luks passed before the class, we were all startled by the sound of a crash of things tumbling, rolling, breaking their way down the stairway. With his usual spontaneous humor, Luks had the mystery solved. He said, with a wave of his hand and a snap of his finger: "Nothing to get frightened about—that's just one of Max Weber's abstract ideas falling down the stairs." It had been Weber's first season as an instructor at the Art Students League.

October 15, 1934

There has been a noticeable decrease of "big bad wolves" disguised in art dealers' clothing. The lengthy depression period has caused their misfit clothes to become shabby and worn out. This condition has enabled sincere artists and art patrons to recognize them by their wagging tales.

The art dealer whose right it is, can and will and must survive, continue to serve and, therefore, to thrive, by reason of his art education, experience and reputation for honesty.

November 1, 1934

Painting boldly, freely and ignorantly is often on a par with loud, noisy orators who are neither inspired, prepared or equipped for their tasks. An idea completely thought out and planned develops that kind of force which people so often refer to as great impromptu orations.

Just as there is a difference between being declamatory and noisy, so a painter, in order to have his canvas make sense, must think things out before he bangs brush marks boisterously into formless blotches of discordant blurs.

November 15, 1934

A rose is a rose because it is not a daisy; and a daisy is a daisy because it is not a rose. And just as there is a difference between a beer stein, a Holstein and a Gert Stein, so is there a difference between a modernist, an ultra-modernist and a faddist.

The artist of today, who is willing and self-satisfied enough to paint in the tradition of the popular discordant art fad of the moment, must of necessity pattern his mental make-up after the method used by the popular song writer or ballyhoo lecturer. He must keep abreast of the changing fetish of novelty in art, closely watching the aesthetic chameleon, performing a constant transition in point of view to suit the current fabricated fashion in art.

December 1, 1934

There is no place for insincerity in art. Therefore, those groups trying to cultivate a sense of art appreciation will do artists and their communities a great service when they learn to feel, as well as to see, in art, earnestness of purpose, or the lack of it,—more plainly, the difference between faking and creating!

Otherwise, our more recently developed art-conscious communities may run the risk of producing, and overproducing, a class of artists who may unwittingly become just so many more picture manufacturers.

Since it has been proven many times that majorities are not always right, let us keep ever alert against the curse of a mediocre majority rule within the art-loving world, which is a relatively small percentage of the general population.

December 15, 1934

Why did Europe eventually accept the paintings and etchings of Whistler, the sculpture of Jacob Epstein, the architectural creations of Frank Lloyd Wright, the music of Foster, the poetry of Poe, the novels of Sinclair Lewis, the plays of O'Neill? Only because the Europeans found the works of these Americans worthy and acceptable.

No matter how firm a transcendentalist one may permit oneself to become, he cannot with any sense of fairness shoot such a "Bullet" as, "the reason Europe won't accept our art is we have nothing acceptable." On the contrary, I find myself one among many who think our home-grown product in art is something to brag about!

January 1, 1935

Freud is not spelled f-r-a-u-d. Painters who want to pass as surrealists are as much in error as the Pseudo-Surrealists, who, in turn, pose as Freudians. Naivete is a charming quality, but it should never be confused with that which is naively neurological.

When some of the more recent perversions of Surrealism are referred to as fads or isms, protests are shrieked about the conservative aloofness for things novel in art. Ballyhooed-Non-Intelligibility in Art is way down from $4,000 to $400 on the auction block. What next? The guillotine?

January 15, 1935

It has been said of Beethoven, the longer he worked on a composition, the fresher and more spirited it became. This thought brings to mind the working methods of the masters, old and modern. Briefly summed up, their modus operandi hides the travail of their creations by absorbing the labored knowledge acquired. Having cultivated a system of sound mental digestion, the accumulated data are allowed to simmer in the artists' minds until filtered by inspiration and fused with the spirit of, and urge for, self expression.

An artist's results are his witnesses.

February 1, 1935

Bravo LaGuardia! Where there is artistic smoke, there must be aesthetic fire. The Mayor and his Municipal Art Committee have the best wishes of all artists and musicians who expect to be benefitted.

To those who walk with the crutches of unstable politics, and rest upon the stumps of outmoded economics, culture lifts its head in meekness, but with no sense of weakness, and says, "Without me you can do nothing." It is high time that conventional blockheads be transformed into stepping stones of a higher order of political, social and cultural administration.

February 15, 1935

He who never does anything never makes any mistakes. The reason why so many of the cuttingly critical in print never produce any bad paintings is due to the fact that they never paint.

The enlightened art critic of today, with his highly developed sensitiveness, has grasped the full significance of the art of criticism. Therefore, he looks more for the silver lining inside of the clouds-upon-clouds of art production, until he finds virtues that over-shadow the many faults of many artists.

March 1, 1935

There are artists who are producing a hybrid art, which is neither a good academic job nor creative work in the sane sense, but rather unharnessed, headstrong, hysterical manifestations upon canvas. Such conduct, when verbally perpetrated, usually lands one in a straightjacket, accompanied with the proper kind of guard, in an institution duly authorized to house the mentally unbalanced.

April 1, 1935

In the majority of cases, a premature urge for display in the galleries exposes the artist's pronounced lack of individuality of concept and succeeds, at best, in reflecting a confusion of influences from other painters.

It is therefore better for the artist, in his formative period, to wait with his wares until both he and his work are a little grown up. How much more expedient it is to know whereof you speak before you ask for an audience!

May 1, 1935

Word wars between contemporary artists should be encouraged. During the process of such thought airings, the more analytical listener will perhaps glean very little. At the time such oratorical or written conflicts take place, confusion may reign. In afterthought, however, when the smoke of the verbal or printed battle has settled into an accountable heap of comparative facts, the workable proofs become mentally digested, and much useful data is later drawn upon and used in one's own way. The open forum method of mass education is always stimulating to the participants as well as to their audiences. It takes the dogma out of art.

June 1, 1935

A cellist and a soprano held forth recently in a joint recital. Since then, a certain group of music lovers have continued to laud the excellent piano playing of the accompanist.

One cannot be too careful in the selection of frames around pictures, especially when the frame becomes a more pronounced work of art than the painting it is supposed to encase for the purposes of aesthetic support. Pictures on exhibition are no different than prima donas on the concert stage.

August 1, 1935

If what you do speaks louder than anything you say, then most certainly the over-production of paintings from the hands of inexperienced, though agitated, artists "hollers" down their verbal volcanic eruptions.

Propagandistic dilettantes, who can neither paint, draw, design nor create, try to hide behind some political "ism" in order to conceal their lack of ability as artists. In some instances they even join the ranks of professional noise-mongers. Occasionally, their tinkling brass brings forth much publicity thunder—without the slightest sign of impending aesthetic showers, nor even the faintest suggestion of a drizzle of artistic innovation. No matter what your medium of expression, if it becomes your goal to do missionary work with a motive to make converts, you must first be possessed of a comprehensive technique.

September 1, 1935

A violin, not made of the right kind of wood and with sound considerations excluded from its construction, will not have any additional value in a hundred years, nor even in a thousand.

So it is with anxious writers on art who suffer from chronic poverty of thought. In their helplessness, they find it necessary to resort to abuse and insult, thus proving that the lower state of mind finds it easier to scoff than to understand. Their mental make-up, like the common wood of the cheap violin, never improves. The love of authority is not enough; therefore, unqualified authoritarians and their writings are short lived.

December 1, 1935

James Boswell and Samuel Johnson sat next to each other at a music hall concert. The furiously flat and foul notes of a member of the company soon aroused the big-boyishness of Boswell, who thought himself not a bad hand at giving animal imitations. He suddenly let loose a perfect cow's "Moo" that brought forth a gale of laughter from the bored audience. This imitation was followed by one of a braying horse, which caused Dr. Johnson to lean over and whisper, "Not so good." Next Boswell emitted rasping sounds mildly resembling the crow of a rooster, at which the Doctor sagely counseled, "Stick to the Moo, Boz."

We extract from this experience a law of relativity for creative workers in any of the fine arts—we all fare better when we stick to our Moo!

January 15, 1936

Any self-styled art expert who pronounces himself an "official art destroyer," just because he happens to be a school principal, should be informed publicly that vandalism becomes not one tittle less destructive though an attempt be made to label the misdeed legal. "G" men cannot be summoned to cope with pretenders in art. But those who know the significance of higher art standards by reason of proven experience should not remain silent and acquiescent to aggressive mismanagement and blind leadership when progress in art is at stake.

May 1, 1936

There are those who know how to draw, and those who know how to see; those who feel interpretively, and those who depend entirely upon their physical eyes and free-hand draftsmanship.

The underlying success of the great modern masters of mental, emotional and technical innovation is an open secret. They are at heart the eternal students, never ceasing to experiment. They are not like those smug professionals, whose study periods come to an end when they have obtained from some educational institution a receipted bill, in the form of a diploma.

September 1, 1936

The sophomoron usually builds up a code of his own for the sole purpose of scoffing at all those who do not conform with his distorted perspective of life and experience. He tries to veneer his vicious cynicism with a lacquer of philosophy. The quick-cracking nature of this type of pseudo-intellectual varnish exposes a primed undercoating of bitterness mixed with secret revenge for fear of impending personal failure.

Only one possessed with this sort of attitude greets everyone he meets with a tirade of alibis about the other fellow's success and apologies for his own unnoticed supposed talents. Sophomoronism finds a lodging place in the minds of those who refuse to grow up mentally.

October 15, 1936

There does not seem to be any doubt that Frans Hals was a beer drinker of quantity. Nevertheless, not every artist who over-indulges in the brewed beverage thereby attains the heights of Hals in depicting tavern life and expressing the spirit of the cup that cheers.

The same can be said of Whistler and publicity. James Abbott MacNeil Whistler, American artist laureate, was his own best press agent. However, all the press-agentry in the world is of small avail when genius and talent do not exist.

November 1, 1936

"The well-read man!" Do you know him? He can quote everybody and anybody. I mean the man upon whom it never dawns to nurse an idea of his own or try to develop it.

There are prototypes of this man among well-informed painters. With apparent technical ease, they strike off a few canvases, with almost perfect mimicry, of this or that school of thought. They "play ball" with the expressive individuality of others without realizing that as separate identities they are at liberty to reflect creative impulses that coincide with their own experiences—and thus accrue far greater acumen in the direction of originality.

November 15, 1936

Procrastination crawls like a thief in the night into many a consciousness, and spurts from its fangs an anesthetic which numbs the will for self-expression. Experimenting and studying as an artist, and acquiring experience as a man—these two qualities, put together and shaken well, make a concoction known as progress.

The alert ones, responsible for the sincere art of today, therefore, come forth with art communications that dare to do, in ways that are new. Ballyhoologically speaking, those who mistake notoriety for fame wave the flag of P. T. Barnum, but instead of a show produce the sounding brass of a counterfeit performance.

March 15, 1937

Aimless jazz painting manifests disorder, discord and chaos. Jazz music has, to say the least, aimed to make the feet move. The period from jazz to swing time embraces a multitude of rhythm, design and much creative stepping.

In popular music, you can swing it without reservations. You can even sing it with neurotic screams and hesitations.

When it comes to artists' paint, you can't swing it because you just can't sling it. Paint is not a vehicle to make the feet move, unless one slips on it.

January 15, 1939

The absence of the creative element in artistic endeavor results in the soul-less, spiritless rendering of the camera eye.

Pictures, music, poems or plays, and especially art criticism, may be mechanically perfect and still remain a prosaic delineation—artless. They who pass off artless documented technique as works of art, only tend to encourage more pot-boilers to invade and adulterate the field of fine arts.

Like the counterfeit man, "They are of short duration and full of trouble."

February 1, 1939

An amateur art collector and dealer (now out of business) once questioned the authenticity of the signature on an etching brought to him by the etcher himself. This artist was obliged to confess, "I signed this one myself. My wife usually signs the edition for me."

Does the graphic artist sell his art or his autograph? The logical answer seems to be that he offers both for sale.

Following up on the well received article about Luks that appeared in February, 1934, Kruse wrote a piece based on his experiences with John Sloan. This article, which appeared in the June-July issue of *Studio News,* had a more serious tone and more theoretical content than the Luks piece. In describing Sloan's teaching methods, Kruse stressed that Sloan urged continual experimentation, "unceasing through self discovery, self analysis and constant self correction."

Sloan was also quoted as advising: "Preserve the memory of the feeling and emotion you had when you conceived what you desired to paint…This is unquestionably a precious thought that no artist can afford to ignore or dispense with after the workable content of the thought is digested." Kruse stated that he had adopted these principles for guidance in his own artistic endeavors.

Elaborating further on the principles of artistic creativity, Kruse said: "I frankly feel the next quotation [from Sloan's teachings] to be worthy of an artist's memory: 'An artist is a workman who takes things from nature and bangs them into the shapes he desires, making every square inch of his painting busy with interest.'" Kruse lauded Sloan's success in capturing "the particular spirit of the type of life involved."

Commenting on Sloan's street imagery, Kruse said, "it is usually so pulsating with the life of some very special character types that one seldom gives thought to the mechanics of the art, it is so very well done." Although Kruse was writing about Sloan, the tone and content of the article left little doubt that the principles enunciated were being followed by the student as well as by the teacher.

Kruse quoted Sloan: "Don't draw the figure by means of the clothes. Build the clothes by means of the figure."

Kruse's personal notebooks, of which he left many, also contain extensive, insightful thoughts about his favorite preoccupations concerning art and creativity: inspiration, innovation, and "inventive design." The following are just a few samples that deal specifically with what he referred to as modern extremism:

Matisse told Max Weber: "Don't forget nature."

Since it is claimed that breaking with tradition is anarchy, the extremists never broke with tradition because they never had the traditional schooling fundamentals.

Nobody ever painted a masterpiece without having had much basic training and practice in inventive design.

Homebodies. (Drawing).

Visiting. (Drawing).

10
Hectic Middle Years

Writing was just one of a number of facets of Alexander Kruse's capabilities that emerged and gained recognition during the 1930s. At the behest of a cousin who was in the corrugated box business, Alex Kruse turned inventor during the mid-1930s. In observing operations in the manufacture of boxes, Kruse noted the importance of stapling machines used to join pieces of cardboard. He noticed that operations were interrupted frequently when stapling machines jammed or ran out of pre-formed staples. Kruse conceived the idea of building a stapler with a source that consisted of a roll of wire to be fed into a unit that cut the wire and created staples as part of routine operations. He built a working model and was awarded a patent. The invention was turned over to the cousin for further development.

Another Kruse invention was an all-in-one paintbox for field sketching. The single package included a container for tubes of paint and brushes, as well as containers for turpentine and oil. The cover of the box contained a slot into which a standard 12-by-16-inch canvas panel could fit. The box also had a built-in palette. Using an adaptation of this design, Kruse was able to do field sketching without an easel or portable palette.

Another digression from his mainline art career came when Kruse designed, prepared molds for, and supervised casting of a set of brass bookends. Each bookend had a figure holding up a Biblical scroll. The scrolls contained paraphrased and abbreviated versions of the Ten Commandments, five commandments on each bookend. Tiffany and Company offered to buy the casts for the bookends. But Kruse declined because he felt the offer was insufficient. Many sets of bookends were produced and sold privately.

From about 1934 onward, with the Kruses' son in school and with rising concerns about family income as the Depression imposed increasing hardships, Anna Kruse took steps to help provide a steady source of income for the family. Deliberately, she examined opportunities and earnings prospects and determined that it would be profitable to develop a skill related to the punched card accounting machines (forerunners of business computer systems) that were rapidly being installed in business and governmental organizations. Anna went through a brief course at a business college where she learned keypunching. After graduating at the head of her class, she landed a job at the New York Telephone Company. As her expertise built, she was hired as a part-time instructor of evening classes at the same school where she had studied originally.

After a few years with the Telephone Company, Anna decided she could enhance the financial security of her family and herself through a civil service position. Accordingly, she reviewed the format and content of civil service tests and began sitting for examinations. She qualified as second in a statewide civil service exam and came out at the top of the list for a test given by New York City. In 1936 or 1937, Anna Kruse went to work for the City of New York, where she continued to be employed until about 1964, when she retired following a heart attack. At the time, she was chief tape librarian for the massive computer installation that generated payroll and pension checks for more than 100,000 employees and retirees.

Keypunching experience also helped make Anna an expert typist, a skill she put to good use by assisting with Alex's increasing writing activities. To supplement this skill, she also took courses in manuscript editing, proofreading, and indexing—background that proved useful in later collaboration with her husband.

Following publication of his article on Sloan, Kruse himself was the recipient of a serious, complimentary article by a friend and fellow artist.

Frank A. Nankivell, a successful printmaker in his own right and an exceptional craftsman who printed Kruse's etchings and aquatints, wrote an extensive article on Kruse's artistry and methods that was published in the March, 1935, issue of *Prints* magazine. The article was entitled "The Work of Alexander Kruse."

In his creative depiction and interpretation of everyday subjects, Kruse was seen by Nankivell as demonstrating an artistic kinship with Walt Whitman and his poetry. In particular, Nankivell admired Kruse's ability to glean humor in city scenes that others saw as mundane. Kruse's *Buy Cash Cloe's,* for example, shows a second-hand peddler who buys and sells used clothes. In Kruse's print, the peddler brings comic relief to himself and his customers by parading through the neighborhood wearing a half-dozen hats, one on top of the other. In *Second Avenue El,* two passengers, a woman and a man, are in back-to-back seats. Both are leaning back, dozing. A long, curved feather on

Buy Cash Cloe's. (Lithograph).

the woman's hat dips toward the man's nose, threatening to tickle him. *In East Harlem* and *Musical Clown* are happy pictures depicting enjoyment of performances by audiences.

In his article, Nankivell admires Kruse's ability to achieve humor without resorting to exaggeration or nonessential detail. The author also applauds Kruse's ability to find aesthetic subject matter in the urban region that surrounds him, as well as Kruse's resolve to continue to depict American subject matter realistically.

E. C. Sherburne of the *Christian Science Monitor* produced another in what proved to be a series of favorable reviews of Kruse's work in writing about the 1936 Biennial Exhibition of the Whitney Museum of American Art, published on January 31, 1936. The show as a whole featured realistic

Second Avenue El. (Lithograph).

works. Sherburne saw this show as a wholesome change from the "derivations, imitations, and exaggerated abstractions" that swept the art scene in the early 1930s. As one example of a sound representation of the American scene without resort to aesthetic excesses, Sherburne cited Alexander Kruse's entry, *East Side Athletic Club* (later renamed *Amateur Bout*). This lithograph, which shows a boxing match, also pictures the reactions caught on the faces of hundreds of spectators. He felt that this picture could "speak for itself as social comment without overaccenting either the action of the boxers or the expression of the spectators."

At the One Hundred Eleventh exhibition of the National Academy of Design held in March and April, 1936, Kruse's lithograph *Eternal Bouquet* was accepted and shown.

Later that year, Kruse participated in the Twenty-first Annual of the American Society of Etchers, held in November and December. His humorous etching, *Buy Cash Cloe's* was shown.

At the Tenth Annual Exhibition of American Block Prints, held in December, 1936, at the Wichita (Kansas) Art Museum, two Kruse works were displayed: *Here Comes the Bride* and *The King of Jazz.*

Significant levels of recognition and publicity resulted from a portrait by Kruse during 1936. The portrait showed New York's Mayor Fiorello LaGuardia conducting the Goldman Band in Central Park in the summer of 1935. Kruse was moved to do the painting in appreciation of the active support for the arts that had been promoted by LaGuardia. The portrait was presented to the Mayor by a Kruse friend and client, I. A. Hershmann, vice president of Sachs Fifth Avenue and head of the New York City Music Project during which LaGuardia performed. Eventually, the painting was donated to the University of Arizona, of which LaGuardia was an alumnus.

In 1937, Kruse took part in an international interchange program arranged through cooperation between the Society of American Etchers and its counterpart in Sweden. A National Exhibition of Contemporary

American Prints was assembled and shown in January, then shipped to Sweden for display. Kruse had two prints accepted for this show, *Young Smoker* and *Forest Park*. Then, at the end of 1937, the Society of American Etchers combined its annual show with a National Exhibition of Contemporary Swedish Prints. The Exhibition, held at Rockefeller Center, included Kruse's *The Ford's End*.

January, 1937, proved to be something of a banner month. While the Sweden-bound show was in progress, Kruse also was represented at the Tenth Annual Exhibition of the Philadelphia Society of Etchers and Graphic Artists. Two Kruse prints were accepted at the Philadelphia show: *Young Smoker* and *Second Avenue El*.

In March of 1937, Kruse's *Squatters* was shown at the Eighteenth International Print Makers

The Mayor Conducts. (Oil).

Exhibition at the Los Angeles Art Museum. Another Spring, 1937, activity in which Kruse participated was the American Block Print Exhibition. This show was staged at the Wichita Museum and was sponsored by the Kansas State Federation of Art. Kruse had four prints in this show: *Here Comes the Bride, Friendly Neighbors, Preparing the Sabbath,* and *The King of Jazz.* After the Wichita showing, this collection was circulated throughout Kansas.

By 1937, socially conscious and liberal activists in the New York area were rallying in support of the Loyalist cause in the Spanish Civil War. Among his activities at this time, Kruse created a portrait (etching) of Spain's King Alphonse, the figurehead of the Loyalist movement. The print was exhibited at several shows held during this period. Within the same time frame, Kruse completed *Two Generations*, a large tempera painting that made an early statement about the forthcoming danger represented by Hitler and the Nazis. It portrays a large kangaroo with the face and military helmet of Kaiser Wilhelm, the German leader during

World War I, carrying a baby-sized Adolph Hitler in its pouch.

Kruse followed his *Two Generations* protest work with an oil called *Espanolaphone*. This shows a bull, as a symbol of Spain, equipped with a telephone earpiece at one end and a mouthpiece at the other. Communicating through this Spanish symbol are Hitler and Mussolini.

Kruse also participated in an ambitious undertaking called the Exhibition in Defense of World Democracy, held at the end of 1937. This show was staged under the auspices of the Second American Artists' Congress, an event in which some 400 artists participated. The Congress, which was a mass meeting in Carnegie Hall to show support for the Loyalist cause, attracted an audience estimated at 2,500. A keynote speaker at the Congress was Erica Mann, Thomas Mann's daughter, who urged listeners to participate in the struggle against Fascism. Pablo Picasso, who had recently been appointed to head the Prado Museum in Madrid, cabled to let attendees know that the Loyalist government had adequately provided for the protection of the Museum's art treasures.

My Mother. (Plaster Cast of Bas Relief in Clay).

The art works in the Exhibition included a set of Picasso etchings caricaturing Franco. Among the American artists who contributed works were Max Weber, William Gropper, and Alexander Kruse, who showed *Two Generations*. In a review of the Exhibition, *Time* magazine cited *Two Generations* as a favorite among the union members who attended the Congress in large numbers.

This same Congress also passed a resolution asking the federal government to continue and increase funding for the WPA artists' project. The WPA, or Works Progress Administration, was a government program designed to put people to work chiefly through major public works such as roads, bridges, and public buildings. However, the WPA also allocated some funds for the creation of art works, photographic exhibitions, and a theatrical production program. Although Kruse did not seek regular employment in the WPA project, he did prepare three lithographs under the auspices of the program. Prints from these were donated to schools and used to create traveling exhibits. Two of these, *Friendly Neighbors*, and *Jennie*, were included in an exhibit at the Cornell Fine Arts Museum, Rollins College, Winter Park, Florida, in 1989. The show was entitled "Works Progress Administration Masters: Prints From the New York Federal Arts Project 1935-41."

In 1938, the Kruse family suffered a major loss and was plunged into sadness by the death of Lena Kruse at 76. Alex's mother had suffered for many months prior to her passing with colon cancer. Alex undertook several projects that showed his determination to create memorials to preserve the memory of his mother. He broke with longstanding Jewish tradition by creating a bas relief sculpture which was cast in bronze and affixed to her tombstone. He also created a series of art collections incorporating his work as well as donated works from many of his friends. These collections were donated to museums and universities across the country under the name of Lena Kruse Memorial Collection. As part of this effort, collections of prints were donated to the Bibliotheque Nationale in Paris, as well as the British Museum and the Victoria and Albert Museum in London.

Lena Kruse's passing also made a major difference in the Kruse family lifestyle. Lena had been the main source of affection and care for Ben Kruse for a number of years, particularly after Anna started to work outside the home. After her death, Alex made special efforts either to take Ben with him if he could conduct his business after school hours or to be at home for his son as much as possible. The years from 1938 through 1942, when Ben entered college at sixteen, added to the already close relationship between father and son.

Homage to Lena Kruse continued when Kruse's collaborators agreed to dedicate the book, *Two New Yorkers,* published in 1938 "To the Memory of L. K." Dust jacket copy proclaimed the book to be "without parallel in publishing history." This, at least, was the view of Stanley Burnshaw, instigator, editor, and driving force behind the project. The end product was a small book with less than fifty pages that matched works of a poet and an artist who had similar backgrounds and similar outlooks—and who shared a close friendship with Burnshaw—Alexander Kruse and Alfred Kreymborg.

Burnshaw and Kruse had become close friends while they worked together on the *New Masses*. Burnshaw was a poet, biographer, essayist, and literary person who co-founded the small publishing company, Bruce Humphries, Inc., that published *Two New Yorkers*. Although Kruse and Kreymborg had never met before they were brought together for the book project, Burnshaw was impressed by similarities in their backgrounds and in the topical focus of their creative work. Both had grown up on the Lower East Side. Both had cigar-maker fathers. Most important, Kruse and Kreymborg shared a devotion to subject matter of urban realism. Burnshaw, also a poet, shared the interest of his friends in urban topics, as evidenced by his contribution of one of the poems in the book for which he saw a close affinity with a Kruse etching.

Burnshaw's introduction indicates that the book "brought together fourteen specimens each from a poet and a painter who scarcely know each other and...made this fusion a book in its own right..." He continues: "The similarities in the idioms of Kreymborg and Kruse could scarcely escape anyone familiar with their work—similarities more serious than the identity of their initials. The curious analogies in their early lives, their fathers' occupations (both cigar makers), their creative approaches, their occupation of the same neighborhood in Manhattan, even identities in personal idiosyncrasies, frequently flashed into my mind. It seemed only logical to bring the two men together."

Dust jacket statements of praise for the book's content came from important literary figures and critics of the day, including Burton Rascoe, William Rose Benet, Carl Zigrosser, Jerome Klein (art critic, *The New York Post*), Emily Genauer (art critic, *The New York World-Telegram*), and Peyton Boswell, Jr. (editor, the *Art Digest*).

Publication of *Two New Yorkers* served, in part, to enrich the intense friendship between the Kruses and Stanley Burnshaw and his wife, a relationship that had a direct effect on the enlargement of Alex Kruse's creative opportunities and subject matter. Through this association, Alex gained access to the rural and pastoral scenic areas that provided subject matter for many of his paintings, an influence apparent in his work throughout his mature years.

In 1936, the Burnshaws had invited the Kruses to spend several weeks at their vacation cabin in Maine. The experience proved mind expanding for Alex Kruse, the perennial city boy. He came back from that summer with a number of canvases showing nearby farms. More important, he enhanced his visions of agricultural scenic composition to encompass complex landscapes.

During much of 1937 and 1938, when Lena Kruse was ill, the Kruses did not take a vacation. However, by 1939, the Burnshaws had set up a summer living pattern that the Kruses shared with enthusiasm. The Burnshaws bought a seven-room house in Briarcliff Manor, New York. The location was on the outskirts of Tarrytown. The address of the Burnshaw's place was on Sleepy Hollow Road, made famous a century earlier in the stories of Washington Irving. During each summer from 1939 through 1941, Alex Kruse spent several weeks absorbing this beautiful environment and producing some memorable landscapes which were well accepted in New York galleries in succeeding years.

Another rural venue opened for Alex and Anna Kruse in 1938, discovered when they drove up to Pawling, New York, to pick up Ben and his friend, Donald Diamond, following a Christmas, 1937, vacation. The two boys, close friends, had been taken by the Diamonds to spend several days on a farm run by Tessie Ackerman, a Hungarian immigrant and widow who supported herself by taking in boarders. When Alex and Anna picked up the boys at the end of their holiday stay, they fell in love with the countryside and the scenery, and were attracted by the reasonableness of Tessie's rates for guests (as well as her excellent cooking). Thereafter, Pawling became and remained a favorite spot for year-round weekends and short vacations.

Over a period of years, the Kruses enjoyed many visits to Pawling with Anna's cousins and their close friends, Dr. Wilbur Sachs and his wife, Jewell. "Willie" Sacks proved to be a loyal friend, good company, and a serious admirer of Alex's work, of which he acquired nine paintings.

Pawling was the kind of friendly place where you met people on the road and invited or were invited to visit. One such friendship was struck with Louis and Betty Pelletier, who made Pawling their full-time home and who enjoyed both the Kruses' company and Alex's artistry. Pelletier was an experienced and successful writer-dramatist. For fifteen years, he wrote all scripts for the radio drama, "The FBI in Peace and War." During the 1960s, the Pelletiers migrated to Los Angeles shortly before the Kruses went West to visit their son and his family. Pelletier, who had an extremely successful Hollywood career that included writing six movie scripts for Walt Disney, helped make the Kruses feel at home later, after they moved to Los Angeles.

Following publication in late 1938, *Two New Yorkers* received relatively heavy promotion and was extensively and favorably reviewed in the New York press. This success was followed shortly by an important appointment that helped build Kruse's reputation as a writer and critic. Beginning in September, 1939, he served as art critic for the *Brooklyn Eagle*, contributing a regular column to the paper's Sunday section.

As a practicing, exhibiting artist, Kruse brought a unique viewpoint to his criticism, adopting an approach that built a professional respect far beyond the local circulation of the *Eagle*. He saw his weekly column as an opportunity to help educate the reading public about art. That is, he wrote for the average reader, not for an inner circle of dilettantes.

To achieve this purpose, Kruse felt it important to avoid tearing down the good name or to impugn the integrity of any artist or exhibitor. Always, he framed his reviews toward building an understanding of what an artist was trying to say, no matter how strongly he, himself, might disagree personally with the intent or content of the works shown. Thus, though he was a serious realist himself, Kruse always wrote reviews that captured the purpose of a piece or a group of works from the point of view of the artist's intended purpose and message. This approach made Kruse many friends

Joseph Stella. A.Z. Kruse (Oil).

Joseph Stella. (Drawing).

among those he reviewed, a feat unusual in itself for a critic working for a big-city paper.

Possibly the most dramatic example of how a critic and the subjects of his reviews can develop mutual appreciation and approval lies in the relationship that grew between Alexander Kruse and Joseph Stella. On the surface, there seems to be little similarity or sympathy between the artistic outlooks of these two men. Stella was an abstractionist; Kruse, a realist. Stella had built his skills and initial reputation on the basis of intense study in Europe with impressionists and early abstractionists. Yet, Kruse, the "creative" realist, admired and considered Stella's *Brooklyn Bridge* series of paintings to be masterpieces of American abstractionism.

Kruse's open admiration of Stella in print dated from a short piece in the *Art Digest* of January 15, 1935, which quoted Kruse's reaction to seeing Stella's work in a group show: "…The king-pin of the show, perhaps, is the self-portrait of Stella as an 'Arab.'" A. Z. Kruse describes the artist's work as being "refined, perfected and developed."

"Joseph Stella," says Kruse, "made his dreams come true by way of powerful lyrics in color, a good while before some present-day inexperienced youngsters claimed to be pioneer painters of dreams. His works sparkle with depth of vision, expressed through inspiring pattern placement. They communicate his general joy in graphically recalling and reliving dreams dreamt and emotions felt. A superior craftsman, he is not bothered with the question of how to do things. This accomplishment leaves him a wider energetic latitude for concern with his thoughts and his feelings."

In one of his early *Eagle* columns, Kruse referred to Stella as "possibly the most electrifying painter in America today." The two men gradually built a mutual respect that blossomed into close friendship, an occurrence that was, in itself, unusual for a critic and an artist. They exchanged a series of letters so noteworthy that, in the 1970s, these documents became the basis for a master's thesis at Valparaiso University in Indiana. One of these letters was a personal appeal by Kruse to Mr. Knoedler that secured a one-man exhibition at Knoedler Galleries for Stella. The exhibition added greatly to Stella's reputation.

Then, in 1941, Stella expressed his friendship and gratitude by painting a portrait of Kruse. Alex Kruse's concern for Joseph Stella and his reputation carried forward even beyond his friend's death in 1946. A nephew who inherited Stella's works came to Kruse for advice. Stella, a highly prolific painter, left a large collection. A dealer recommended destroying some selected canvases to enhance the value of the others. Kruse became incensed. On his advice, the complete body of work was retained, to the art world's great benefit.

During the early 1940s, Kruse wrote about a unique talent he observed in the work of Ellis Wilson, one of the first African-American artists to exhibit in a New York gallery. Following the encouraging review, the men became friends. Later, when Wilson accepted an invitation to the Kruse home (which had transferred to Manhattan by then), the doorman insisted that Wilson enter through the servant's entrance. Kruse became insensed, raising a fuss that didn't end until Wilson was accorded an abject apology and made welcome in the building from then on.

As was true of many other young artists of the day, Ellis Wilson realized direct, tangible benefits from the encouragement and efforts of Alex Kruse, as witnessed in these excerpts from a letter to Kruse, dated April 7, 1944:

"I have just received the news that I have been granted the Guggenheim Award. Needless to say, the news was most welcome and darn sure I will profit greatly from the opportunity this gives me to carry out plans in my work for the coming year.

"I am very grateful indeed for the valuable assistance and sponsorship you have so kindly given me and which I am sure was most instrumental in my receiving the award."

Kruse launched the *Eagle* column at a time when public appreciation and support for art enjoyed a major stimulus due to the presence in town of the New York World's Fair, which ran over three summers from 1939 through 1941. Over the spring and summer of 1940, the New York area came into a full bloom of art showings either at or in connection with the

Albert Hirschfield. Art Critic's Circle.

World's Fair. Kruse's correspondence files bulged with invitations by letter and telegram to attend openings of special events put on by Fair exhibitors, museums, and corporations. Although the invitations made for a busy schedule, each inevitably presented opportunities to meet and mix with persons who were playing important roles in the art world. The experiences were both interesting and reputation-enhancing.

The *Eagle* column quickly evolved into a regular working routine. Every Sunday, Kruse would make up a list of the shows to be covered that week. Monday was his day to make rounds of the galleries. Inevitably he was greeted with warm hospitality. Often, he would encounter fellow critics on these rounds and would pause to chat with both colleagues and old friends. Then he would pick up a catalog for the show and examine the work while he made notes on the catalog. Returning home, he would handwrite his reviews on Tuesday and Wednesday, in time for the column to be typed Wednesday night by Anna and delivered to the *Eagle* on Thursday.

In some of the early columns, errors crept into the paper as Linotype operators stumbled over the strange names of artists or titles of their works. Always a perfectionist, Kruse formed a habit of visiting the paper's composing room on Fridays to proofread his column. Very quickly, he learned the exact position where his column was set up and placed in a page. Not unexpectedly, some of the typographers were ungracious about pulling special proofs for Kruse to read. At first, proofs were felt to be necessary because the metal type was reverse reading—images were backwards from the way the impressions would appear on paper. Ever innovative, Kruse made a habit of bringing a small pocket mirror with him. He would simply hold the mirror over the type as it lay in the page forms and check his copy, calling any errors to the attention of disconcerted but admiring typographers.

One of the more pleasing duties that fell to Kruse as a critic was to review a 1941 retrospective exhibition of Jerome Myers, his late friend and teacher, who died in 1940. The review was much appreciated by Ethel Myers, Jerome's wife.

Another instance of recognition for Kruse came with an event that took place on March 7, 1941. The occasion was a group dinner for sixteen leading art critics who dubbed themselves the "Art Critics Circle." The affair was held in the Margarita Restaurant at 116 East Fifty-ninth Street, long a favorite of Luks, Sloan, Bellows, and others of that group. Host of the event was Nelson Lansdale of *Newsweek*. The event was commemorated by a group caricature by popular cartoonist Albert Hirschfeld of *The New York Times*. The caricature, which ran both in the *Art Digest* (March 15) and *Cue* magazine (March 22), included a lineup of Betty Chamberlin, *Time*; Amee Craft, *Stage*; Peyton Boswell, Jr., *Art Digest*; Emily Genauer, *New York World-Telegram*; Edward Alden Jewell and Howard Devree, *New York Times*; Carlyle Burrows, *New York Herald-Tribune*; Maude Riley, *Cue*; Kruse, Lansdale, Rosamund Frost, *Art News*; Elizabeth McCausland, *Springfield Republican*; and Frank Caspers, *Art Digest*.

In between work on the Sunday column, Kruse continued, without letup, to paint. By 1941, he was concentrating totally on painting because, as described earlier, the printmaking profession virtually died under the onslaught of the cheap prints from Associated American Artists that flooded the market. Weyhe Gallery, which had been a source of both artistic support and financial income, eventually faded out of existence because its artists could no longer subsist in the changing, declining marketplace for prints.

Woodcutter

Morning Prayer

11
Maturity and New Dimensions

In 1941, at 53, Alex Kruse finally reached that rarified plateau in the art world, a point at which he had achieved enough respect as an artist to warrant major one-man exhibitions in addition to the group shows in which he had enjoyed excellent reception for many years. Also, he had reached the level of prestige that translated into recognition as a critic, respect as a teacher, and ready acceptance as a lecturer on art.

In the spring before the United States was drawn into World War II, Kruse had the good fortune to receive an invitation for a major retrospective exhibition from David Findlay, who operated the Findlay Galleries at 69 East Fifty-seventh Street, an excellent location between Fifth and Park Avenues. The catalog noted that the works presented were produced between 1914 and 1941. The show, which opened April 22 and ran through May 10, gave eloquent testimony to Kruse's artistry, virtuosity, and love for the media in which he worked. The catalog listed thirty-six oils, two tempera-and-oil paintings, one pure tempera piece, two pastels, and a charcoal drawing, for a total of forty-two individual works. These, the catalog noted, were in addition to thirty lithographs and etchings. The

TAKING ART TO HEART

On the Fire Escape. (Oil). This was painted from an early sketch of Lena Kruse washing windows at 133 Henry Street.

overall total of seventy-two pieces clearly qualified this as an impressive retrospective. The critics certainly agreed.

Emily Genauer, in her review in the *World-Telegram* of April 26, 1941, wrote: "The oils range from dark, comparatively early, and very good studies of city life, like the 1927 *On the Fire Escape,* 1914 *Young Smoker,* and 1916 *Waiting* to a series of large landscapes in which emphasis is placed on iridescent tone, and a number of very small, unpretentious vignettes of local beaches and docks which, to my mind, are infinitely more pleasing." Genauer found that, "a late canvas, carefully and dramatically composed, called *Cow Barn,* is…the best picture in the exhibit."

Howard Devree reviewed Kruse's Findlay show for *The New York Times.* Devree applauded the long time span covered by the exhibited pieces as well as the love for his subjects apparent in Kruse's work. Devree also praised the work as unpretentious, sound in construction, and executed with a lively sense of color. Specific pieces singled out for mention included *Briarcliff Valley* for its sensitive light greens, *The Mayor Conducts* for the genial humor reflected in the expression that Kruse caught in his subject, and the *Self-Portrait of an Art Critic,* which was seen as libelously amusing. In the latter painting, Kruse depicted himself with horns, long devil's ears, a sinister mask, and a matching devilish grin.

In a review published in the *New York Herald-Tribune,* Carlyle Burrows commented on the visible differences in Kruse's treatment of color, feeling, and composition over the time span covered by the show. Burrows also admired Kruse's versatility and frank realism. Burrows commented that "His [Kruse's] realism is of the honest kind, observant of facts, straightforward in statement—yet a realism not uninfluenced by humor and by poetry. In following Kruse's trend from the *Young Smoker,* one of his earliest works, to the *High and Low Road* of a recent year, one can see how clarification, elaboration of color and the broader pictorial view have aided his development along contemporary lines, and especially in the direction of landscape. Two of his recent farm pictures, the *High and Low Road,* and *McGee's Farm,* bring out the best—in color, feeling and composition—in the exhibition of extremely varied pictorial content." The two farm scenes cited by Burrows were painted in Briarcliff

104

Manor during a summer Kruse spent with the Burnshaws.

Joining with most of the other critics who reviewed the Findlay show, Margaret Breuning of the *New York Journal-American* commented on the courage required for an art critic to expose himself to the potential devastation of criticism by his colleagues. Breuning commented that Kruse had effectively practiced the principles he preached and taught. She cited *Briarcliff Valley, Coney Island Creek,* and *Brooklyn Borough Bridge* as the best pieces in design and simplified statement.

Charles Z. Offin, editor and publisher of *Pictures on Exhibit* magazine, noted that Kruse's Findlay show was one of three then running in which the artist was also a critic. The other two presented the work of Albert Gallatin and Walter Pach. Offin contrasted Kruse's work with the abstract compositions by Gallatin and with Pach's preference for retaining a turn-of-the-century French style. Kruse's style, according to Offin, was executed "always with a penchant for the human approach…[Kruse] knows how to avoid sentimentality and keeps his pictures interesting in design and plastic values."

Since Kruse was unavailable to review the Findlay show for the *Brooklyn Eagle,* Jane Corby was given the assignment. Not a professional artist or critic, Corby concentrated on relating for her readers the locations of Kruse's Brooklyn works and discussing the artist's treatment of familiar neighborhoods. She commented: "From this material, and using color in an unusual way—amethyst light on moss-grown stones, for instance—he [Kruse] contrives to invest the scenes he chooses with an odd vitality and familiar atmosphere."

Praise on which Kruse placed great personal value also came from a number of practicing artists. One contemporary artist, John Barber, in a handwritten letter dated May 16, 1941, wrote:

"After my second visit to your exhibition, I must give vent to my enthusiasm for your endeavors and accomplishments…I feel you have triumphed in the sense that you have two outstanding qualities so dearly sought by artists. First, you have 'caught' light and placed it in your canvases without having had to resort to the broken color scheme of the Impressionists. And, secondly, your colors have the transparency the great Dutch masters achieved.

"You have reason to continue your life's work with great satisfaction and it gives me great pleasure to send you these few words."

With the closing of the Findlay show, the Kruses were, shortly, faced with the closing of a long, cherished chapter in the life of the family. Sigmund Kruse, who had been failing for some two years, finally expired in the summer of 1941. As he had done with his mother, Alex meticulously crafted a bas relief sculpture of his father, which was affixed to his tombstone prior to an unveiling ceremony the following year.

In 1942, Kruse took on additional duties at the *Eagle*. While he continued his Sunday art reviews, he added periodic feature articles. Combining his talents as he had done for many years, he conducted in-depth interviews with prominent people, producing feature articles accompanied by litho crayon or charcoal portraits of his subjects. Kruse's subjects were civic leaders, many with some ties to industrial, civic, or cultural affairs in and around Brooklyn. Since the columns were introduced after the United States entered World War II, some interviews featured people who were making special contributions to the war effort.

For example, one of the interviews featured Rear Admiral Edward John Marquart, then commander of the Third Naval District. Marquart also functioned as commander of the Brooklyn Navy Yard, an installation that employed more than 40,000 military and civilian personnel to build and maintain ships of war. Kruse's article covered the complex and important duties of the commander, while his portrait showed the decisiveness that was a qualification for the job.

In another war-effort-related article, Kruse interviewed and drew Reginald E. Gillmore, then president and a director of the Sperry Gyroscope Company, the Brooklyn firm that produced the top-secret bombsight that played such an important role in strategic bombing operations by Allied forces. Kruse's article characterized Gillmore as an engineer, inventor, and production expert while the accompanying portrait reflected a man with responsibilities of heroic stature.

Long before the women's movement came to the news forefront, Kruse recognized the uniqueness and talent of Mary Dillon, president of the Brooklyn Borough Gas Company, with an in-depth interview about her experiences and an accompanying portrait.

Always a booster of cultural activities in Brooklyn, Kruse paid tribute to Laurence Page Roberts, director of the Brooklyn Museum, the man credited with raising both attendance and the artistic stature of the institution during his tenure as its leader.

Another culture-promoting subject was James Grover McDonald, an influential news commentator who also served as president of the Brooklyn Institute of Arts and Sciences. Activities covered in Kruse's article included McDonald's contributions as founder of the Foreign Policy Association and organizer of the Brooklyn Symphony Orchestra.

Other community leaders interviewed and drawn by Kruse included Philip A. Benson, real estate and banking leader as well as a renowned art collector; Edward Lazansky, Presiding Justice in the Appellate Division of the Supreme Court and a former Secretary of the State of New York; William Milligan Park, division manager for Goodwill Industries; Reverend Sanford C. Hearn, a Methodist minister who ran the York Street Center, a settlement house serving the Brooklyn Navy Yard area; Edmund Reek, producer of the Fox Movietone News series; and Lew Lehr, an actor who starred in comic shorts for Fox Movietone News.

During the 1940s, Alex and Anna Kruse made several attempts to extend their writing beyond the journalistic and into serious literary works. One project was the development of an autobiographical novel built around experiences of Alex's own youth. To prime themselves for this project, they took college-level courses in fiction writing. They took the commitment seriously enough so that they kept working on the novel, which they called *East of Broadway,* for several years, completing a draft in the late 1940s, then revising it again in the early 1950s.

There was considerable interest, but never a commitment to publish during Alex and Anna Kruse's lifetimes. However, they did leave copies of the manuscript in the effects that passed to their son after Anna's death in 1975. The manuscript languished for a number of years. However, in 1992, it was resurrected and put back into work. Benedict Kruse had acquired some fifty years of experience as a writer by then. He edited and did enough revision to satisfy his professional judgment, then brought *East of Broadway* back to the literary marketplace. The book was published and released for marketing in September, 1994, coinciding with a major "rediscovery" exhibition of Alex Kruse's work scheduled for the same month at the R. H. Love Galleries, Chicago.

During the 1940s. Alex and Anna Kruse also collaborated on a proposal for another literary project. They applied to the Ford Foundation for a grant to enable Alex to write a biographical review of the work of the American Eight. He proposed to prepare a manuscript that would reflect his intimate knowledge of the people and their works. At the time of the proposal, Sloan and Shinn were still alive and would have been available for interviews that would have added to Kruse's own rich and detailed background. Unfortunately, the proposal was turned down.

Alex Kruse had a sense of destiny about both his own work and the art of the people he respected. From Sloan, Luks, and Henri, he had learned to be meticulous about preparations for painting and about the care of canvases. For example, he always bought supplies of linseed oil well in advance of his immediate needs. Then he would place bottles of the oil on a window ledge where they would be exposed to bright sunlight. He would continue to store them this way for at least a year to allow the sun to bleach the oil so that it would not darken after he used it for painting.

Most of the canvases he created before the family moved out of Brooklyn were subjected to a mounting procedure he devised to help assure permanence. He would affix the canvas to a panel of Masonite that had been treated with a white lead paint to keep it from corroding. To do this, Kruse applied a casein glue that he had mixed himself to both the panel and the back of the canvas. After the canvas was placed against the treated panel, heavy weight would be used to keep it in place until the glue was thoroughly dry. In its final stage, the procedure took on an almost comical look; the canvas and the panel to which it adhered would be placed on the Kruse's dining-room table and a series of chairs and other heavy objects would be placed on top to assure a tight bond. The process was not easy; but it did add to the permanence of the paintings.

The work associated with writing his art criticisms and preparing illustrated interviews did not deter Kruse from his primary activities as a productive, creative artist and active exhibitor. In 1942, Kruse took part in a Whitney Museum show entitled "Between Two Wars: Prints by American Artists 1914-1941." Kruse's old friend, Carl Zigrosser, was curator for this show. By this time, Zigrosser had become curator of prints at the Philadelphia Museum of Art. In the catalog for this show, Zigrosser expressed his feeling that the art of printmaking had reached maturity in America before either painting or sculpture. The Kruse lithograph, *Young Smoker,* hung in a gallery in company of works of a number of colleagues, including Reginald Marsh, Kenneth Hayes Miller, Peggy Bacon, Isabel Bishop, Yasuo Kuniyoshi, and George Biddle.

The friendship with Zigrosser continued warmly through the years even though they saw each other infrequently. In his diary for May 17, 1967, in Los Angeles, Alex wrote:

> ...We bused to the L.A. Art Museum—primarily to hear Carl Zigrosser lecture on Graphic Art with slides. It was a spirited reunion between us—Mrs. Zigrosser took up well with Ann. Carl did a very good job—considering the limited time allowed. The number of slides had to be limited. But then the field of graphic art is so vast—starting from primitive days in the upward climb of centuries past—it is the enjoyable activity of a lifetime.

Kruse also was represented, in 1942, in the Twenty-sixth Annual of the Brooklyn Society of Artists. His small painting, *On the Fire Escape,* was shown. This piece had special sentimental value for the Kruse family, since it was based on a sketch Alex had prepared while the family lived at 133 Henry Street. The subject was Lena Kruse standing on a fire escape cleaning windows.

In 1943, Kruse participated in the First National Exhibition of Prints hosted by the Library of Congress. His work was also included in the Artists for Victory show held at the Metropolitan Museum of Art in 1943. Another 1943 showing in which Kruse was represented was the Twenty-seventh Annual of the Brooklyn Society of Artists. This show was the last in which Kruse participated as a Brooklyn artist.

In 1944, Alex and Anna Kruse finally left Brooklyn, a move they had contemplated for some time. A change in lifestyle was due. Lena and Sigmund were gone. Ben had been spending most of his time in a rented room near Columbia University, which he had entered in the fall of 1942. In 1944, Ben left for the Army, leaving Alex and Anna with a house that was too large and too empty, particularly in light of the activity patterns into which they had evolved. Anna was working full time in Manhattan. Alex's activities centered around the galleries, most of which were on Fifty-seventh Street or in that immediate Manhattan vicinity. Alex also turned fifty-six in 1944, an age at which his enthusiasm for shoveling snow and other such household responsibilities was diminishing.

In late spring of 1944, Alex and Anna Kruse cleaned out the accumulated trappings of twenty-one years of residence in the Brooklyn house and moved to a two-room apartment at 54 Riverside Drive at the corner of Seventy-eighth Street. The apartment boasted a view of the Hudson River and had a bedroom with a north light, an ideal location for Alex to set up an easel and to carry on a prolific schedule of painting. The War was on and, with a number of galleries closed for the duration (some because proprietors like David Findlay were in military service), exhibition activities were minimal. The Kruses continued to visit Pawling regularly. A number of portrait commissions came to Alex, partly because the war was separating family members and creating a desire for remembrances.

Many longtime friends and family members of the Kruses lived in the new West Side neighborhood or within travel ranges that were a lot closer than from the Brooklyn location. In particular, George and Carrie Medalie lived just eight blocks away up Broadway. The Kruses' new location proved ideal for Carrie Medalie, an enthusiastic walker who became a frequent visitor and who felt comfortable with the Kruses' informality and with the ability to drop in unannounced without upsetting anyone. Carrie Medalie, wife of a Supreme Court Judge, was also an influential person around New York in her own right. She was Secretary of the New York City Board of Higher Education, which oversaw the city's growing college system. Carrie Medalie was an astute follower of the stock market and a shrewd investor. Her investment advice helped bring the Kruses a greater measure of financial security than they had ever known previously.

Early in 1946, Alex Kruse, along with members of his extended family and most of the political establishment in New York State, were grieved over the sudden, untimely death of George Medalie. At the time, Judge Medalie was at the peak of his political power. With Franklin Roosevelt dead and Harry Truman being treated as a laughingstock, it appeared certain that Thomas E. Dewey was destined to be the next President of the United States. Medalie's sudden death cut off what appeared at the time to be a certain appointment to one of the country's top political jobs in Washington. One aftermath of George's death was an increased closeness between the Kruses and Carrie Medalie, who became a regular guest for Sunday night dinner in the Kruse home, a practice that persisted for many years.

The end of the War in 1945 was followed, all too soon, by the end of the *Brooklyn Eagle,* which had fallen victim to wartime and postwar inflation. Like a number of other daily newspapers, *Eagle* management found themselves unable to meet the union demands that reflected wage scales that, in some cases, tripled during the War years. With the news stimulus provided by the War gone, and with increasing competition from radio news, a medium that had come into its own during the War, the *Eagle* was simply unviable economically.

However, the post-War period created new conditions that were quickly converted to opportunities for Alex Kruse. During the War, many educational careers and artistic interests were suspended as people became involved in round-the-clock requirements to boost production, to conserve resources through stringent civilian rationing, and generally to minimize nonessential activities. Art became both a serious pursuit and a popular pastime as museums, colleges, and community institutions began offering programs to satisfy what proved to be a pent-up demand following the cultural hiatus during the War.

Alex Kruse always had great empathy with anyone who enjoyed painting and who turned to art for creative fulfillment. After World War II, and after the *Eagle* stopped publishing, he looked for opportunities to teach art, a love that he had pursued for some forty years. One of his first connections, and his most widely accepted program, came through the Brooklyn Museum. Recognizing the opportunity to help working people or students who wanted to pursue their art activities on weekends, he developed special classes for the "Sunday Painter." The Brooklyn Museum appointed him to teach its first class of Sunday painters. He gave his students a varied experience, picking a wide range of sites throughout Brooklyn where the group would meet on Sundays.

In this and the many other teaching activities in which Kruse engaged after the War, he returned to his basic beliefs. He would set up a portable easel alongside those of the students. He followed the same basic approach that Sloan and others had used in his own instruction; Alex Kruse believed in teaching through demonstration. However, he also took great care not to dictate style or vision for his students. Each student was treated as an individual. Kruse and a student would discuss a canvas in terms of the student's own vision and purpose. The teacher's assistance would be adjusted accordingly.

During 1946, Kruse also accepted assignments to teach at the Master Institute of United Arts, part of the Riverside Museum, and at the McBurney YMCA. He also taught illustration at the Cartoonists and Illustrators School.

But his main teaching affiliation for several years remained the Brooklyn Museum, where he accepted appointments to teach increasing numbers of classes. In addition to his Sunday painting class, he also taught advanced and beginning classes in drawing, painting, and composition. Later, his course load at the Museum was expanded to include offerings in portraiture and figure drawing.

By 1950, Kruse had added a series of classes at Brooklyn College to his teaching load. He taught beginning and advanced portrait painting at the College.

For a number of years, beginning in the late 1940s and extending into the 1950s, Kruse taught a summer class in outdoor painting at Pawling, New York. The program was conducted in cooperation with the local summer stock program at the Starlight Theater. Sessions were held on Saturday afternoons and took place outdoors on theater grounds, except when it rained. On rainy afternoons, the class moved indoors to the theater's rehearsal hall.

Alex Kruse and his weekend class at the Starlight Theater, Pawling.

After overcoming many misgivings and following much hesitation, Alex and Anna Kruse finally agreed to ride in an airplane in August, 1947. They had little choice. Their son, Benedict, was getting married to Bettijune Frank, a girl he had met at Columbia and who came from a Detroit family.

During a brief interval in a hectic weekend, arrangements were made for Alex and Anna to visit the Detroit Art Institute, which boasted a number of masterpieces in which Alex had a high level of interest. In particular, Detroit had Peter Breughel the Elder's *Wedding Dance*, which Kruse respected as one of the great painting compositions of all time. Also in Detroit was the excellent mural court that was a masterwork by his friend Diego Rivera.

A major personal and emotional impact on Alex and Anna Kruse's life occurred in September, 1948, with the birth of their first grandchild, Liane Jennifer. They nicknamed her *Lichtekeit,* which they loosely translated from the Yiddish to describe the child as the light of their lives.

Two younger grandchildren, Martin Alexander and Steven Lewis, followed during the next seven years to share their grandparents' bountiful love. Alex and Anna Kruse were natural and enthusiastic grandparents and, as the children grew, the senior and junior Kruses became increasingly close. The intense feelings that developed within Alex are demonstrated in part of a letter he wrote on April 19, 1962, to his son and daughter-in-law, Bettijune. At the time, Alex was recovering emotionally from the shock of having Anna hospitalized with the first of three heart attacks. On learning of his mother's condition, Ben, who was away from home on business, caught the first available plane to New York and stayed with Alex until Anna had recovered sufficiently so his parents could manage on their own. Alex wrote:

"When the heart is full, the mouth overflows. I am therefore tapping my imagination and seeing myself talking to both of you, surrounded by three of the loveliest grandchildren in all the world—Liane, Martin, and Stevie.

"It was so noble of you, Bettijune, to have acted with such electrifying alertness in paging Ben at Chicago immediately after I phoned you. I consider it a Herculian task for Ben to have set aside the business activities he was engrossed in and appear at the hospital at mother's bedside within a scanty few hours…Ben's presence lifted mother's morale immediately…I know I'm sending mother's sentiments in everything I've written."

By 1949, Kruse was back in print with a new newspaper column. For the *New York Post,* he contributed a weekly column to the weekend magazine section. It was called *Art With a small "a"* and was aimed at the casual hobbyist or the person with a general interest in drawing. In a progressive series of lessons, the column provided instruction in the basics of drawing. The lessons were kept simple; the reader needed only pencil, paper, and an eraser to follow Kruse's program.

Although the stated purpose of the *Post* series was instructional, Kruse also used the columns as a soap box for some of his favorite themes about art appreciation. For example, his column of October 21, 1949, used the presence of a major exhibition to impart some important lessons about the need to master the craft of the artist as a basis for applying artistic inspiration. Excerpts from this column follow:

> Let's take time out today for a big league affair, the exhibition of 162 paintings and drawings by Vincent Van Gogh, on view at the Metropolitan Museum of Art.
> Most reading persons are familiar with the tragic story of Van Gogh…What is not so generally known is that Van Gogh copied the works of certain masters whom he held in great esteem. This span of his career should be of special interest to followers of this column…
> Van Gogh evolved his creative technique as a result of what he learned from the Impressionists. The early Impressionists—Manet, Pissarro, and their followers—studied the effect of color as seen through a cut-glass prism with the sun shining through it. They transferred their findings onto canvas in chunks of brilliant complementary colors, juxtaposed one to another.
> Then came the young Georges Seurat, who with dots of color instead of blobs of pigment (Pointillism), achieved the same sunlit result.
> By stretching the color dots into colored lines, Vincent Van Gogh became an innovating Post-Impressionist. His painted surfaces took on a new kind of life…technique was secondary to Van Gogh. It was what he had to say that was of primary importance…All of Van Gogh's paintings were born out of experience.

Kruse's final column in the *Art With a small "a"* series presented a lesson on drawing a male torso. The final drawing in the sequence was the one Alex had used as his own entry in the examination for admission, in 1904, to the National Academy of Design. Then, he encouraged his readers with the following explanation:

> Before entering the Academy, the only other training I had in drawing was acquired at the Educational Alliance Art School in a class for children, held after three, when P.S. 2 was let out. The instructor was Henry McBride, now the dean of American art critics. So you see that those of you who have followed this series regularly are at least as well prepared as I was to draw the full-length male figure.
> I hope I have succeeded in teaching you to teach yourselves. For what advantage is it to keep acquiring knowledge without attempting to make use of what you have already learned?

Early in 1952, Ben Kruse had the good fortune to discover an opportunity for his father. By then, Ben was a freelance journalist and photographer in Chicago. At a convention he attended, Ben learned that Barnes and Noble, the publisher, had initiated a series of "how to" books called the "Everyday Handbook Series." Noting that the publisher had not yet brought out a basic art book, Ben inquired and was able to set up an appointment for his father to visit the New York publisher. A highly successful conclusion ensued when, in 1953, Barnes and Noble published Alexander Kruse's *How to Draw and Paint*. The book used some of the material from the *Post* columns, but these were expanded to create a comprehensive set of instructions designed to impart basic drawing and painting skills for beginners.

Letters of praise used to help with the book's promotion were received from Francis Henry Taylor, director of The Metropolitan Museum of Art, and from James C. Boudreau, dean of the Art School of Pratt Institute. Most general consumer bookstores in the country featured regular displays of the Everyday Handbook Series. Almost all stocked and regularly reordered Kruse's book, for which sales continued for more than twenty years. Eventually, more than 300,000 copies of this book were sold.

In 1955, Kruse produced an even more basic book for beginning artists. The title was *ABC of Pencil Drawing*. As was the case with the *Post* columns, the instruction was limited to projects that could be completed with pencil, paper, and eraser. Step-by-step instructions were provided for the drawing of basic lines and shapes, then followed up with instructions on drawing flowers, landscapes, and people. The publisher of the thirty-two-page booklet, which sold for fifty cents and was widely circulated, was Bartholomew House, Inc.

Starting in 1954 and carrying through to the mid-1960s, Kruse delivered a series of lectures in the New York area, then throughout the East. His lectures fit into two separate categories. The first type of lecture was *about* art. Kruse would lecture on and discuss topics ranging from a general history of art to specific schools of art or individual painters. Often, these lectures were coordinated with exhibitions by galleries or museums. Even though he was a realist, Kruse was able to deal effectively with explanations and/or questions about abstract and non-objective art. His principles remained constant regardless of medium or style: Kruse evaluated the integrity of an artist's vision. As indicated earlier, he was a great admirer of Joseph Stella even though Stella's work was totally different from his own. Much of Picasso's work also drew praise from Kruse. Over time, Kruse developed an understanding for and appreciation of Mondrian's paintings. The same was true for the work of artists like Klee and Kandinsky.

What Kruse had no patience with was imitators and opportunists, people who mass-produced paintings that they believed would have a ready sale. As popular styles changed, so did the works of these imitators. Another of his pet peeves was ultra-large paintings that depict nothing and deliver no discernable message.

Another, entirely different type of lecture involved a portrait demonstration. These were given for sponsoring groups of interested lay people or amateur painters. The lecture would be delivered concurrently with the painting of a portrait of a selected member of the sponsoring group.

These lecture activities were lucrative. Kruse made these presentations interesting enough to be called upon for many appearances before a wide variety of groups. A professional lecture bureau sold and administered this program.

In his lectures, as in his writings, Kruse stressed the value of mastering basic craft-like skills, then embellishing them with innovation. A typical statement:

> In some of my classes at Brooklyn College, I teach copying of old and modern masters, but not as it was taught to me. I stress interpretive, rather than facsimile, copying. This is one sure way of getting into the habit of thinking and painting creatively.
>
> Here's an example of what I mean. My students consist of adults engaged in the usual and generally accepted variety of occupations. One of my most industrious and enthusiastic pupils was a middle-aged tailor. Not long ago, I assigned to this student a reproduction in color from a Cezanne still-life for him to copy. It was a simple study of a vase containing a few flowers. I got the student started on making his copy, then left him on his own while I circulated among the rest of the pupils in the class. By the time I got back to the tailor for his second criticism, I found that he had painted a complete bouquet on his canvas, instead of the scanty few flowers in that Cezanne print.
>
> "How come?" I asked.
>
> "Well, I'll tell you," he confided. "To me, Cezanne's still-life looked too empty, as though it needed something else in it, so I figured and figured, and decided what it needed was a couple of extra flowers. It's a big improvement, isn't it?"
>
> So you see this part-time artist…deviated widely enough from the print to create an arrangement with a life of its own. And who knows? If Cezanne were alive, he might even have patted him on the back. On the other hand, he might have broken that canvas over the tailor's head.
>
> Whatever the pros and cons, I think everyone is agreed that art, like the institution of marriage, is here to stay, and with no less an interesting variety of consequences.
>
> Perhaps the best known amateur painters in the world today are President Eisenhower and Sir Winston Churchill. But there have been others. Many years ago, a bank clerk took up art as a hobby. But, when the urge to paint became stronger than he was, there was no question or doubt in his own mind as to which activity he would sacrifice—his steady income or his art. Paul Gauguin made his choice and the rest is modern art history.

The art of which Grandma Moses is perhaps the best exponent manifests a pleasant, child-like quality; it is cheerful in color and...despite its faulty painting and errors in structure, this type of art-by-instinct is, at times, as charming as melodic folk music. In any case, it cannot be denied that this form of popular painting is, at its best, far more zestful than the dead copies of live objects which literal, academic painters all too frequently turn out...

Technical perfection, in and of itself, can never camouflage uninspired and soul-less painting. That is why we are only too willing to make concessions and allowances for any work which reveals the slightest degree of fantasy and imagination.

Anecdotes about Kruse's experiences as an art critic were always popular on the lecture circuit. Some examples:

One day, I came into a gallery in which there was only one other person, a young woman to whom I didn't give a second glance, if I can get you to believe that. As I went about my business, walking around the picture-filled room making notes in the margin of my catalog...this tall, simply dressed woman trailed along beside me and tried very discreetly to peek over my shoulder to see what I was writing.

After about fifteen minutes of this curiosity dodging, my work at that gallery was finished...Just then, the director came out of his office, beamed at me and said: "I see that you and Miss Garbo know each other."

Yes, it was Greta herself. [She] explained that the artist whose work I was reviewing was a friend of hers and she was extremely anxious to get my reaction to the paintings but hadn't the nerve to ask me point blank.

At the Museum of Modern Art, I ran across an elderly couple one day who were standing before one of those multiple profiles by Picasso. This particular head had two noses, a superfluous eye, and an ear to spare. The woman, staring at this painting, shrugged her shoulders and shook her head in bewilderment. But the man was more articulate. He banged his cane on the floor and exclaimed, "That's not a face. That's spite work."...

We must understand that Picasso regards an eye, nose, or ear merely as a bit of pattern, interrelated to all of the other shapes he chooses to install, in a U-turn sort of way, within the rectangle of his canvas. In his defense, it must be said that, appearances to the contrary, there is little deliberate chaos in Picasso's work. Every stroke is carefully planned, even though his design inventions are not always obvious at first glance...

It is lucky that Picasso, with his uncontrollable urge for dynamic design experimentation, is an artist instead of a surgeon.

Robert Henri...always urged his students, "Say what you have to say, no matter how crudely—but say it." In other words, get in the first impression, no matter how incomplete, then draw upon your technical knowledge to carry out your initial inspiration.

In 1960, the *Brooklyn Eagle* experienced a brief revival. An investor group bought rights to the name and files, then started to publish in the belief that the new printing technologies that had emerged since 1946 would make the venture financially feasible. The startup was fortuitous, corresponding with a general newspaper strike that shut down all of the regular New York City papers. Business boomed for the weeks while the strike lasted, with copies of the *Eagle* in demand throughout the New York metropolitan area and advertising revenues far surpassing initial projections. When the strike was settled, the paper failed to maintain the readership necessary to interest advertisers, particularly in the face of growing competition from television. Through the tenure of the revival, Kruse returned to writing a weekly column of art criticism.

For a number of years following World War II, Kruse hesitated to deal with New York galleries. He was disillusioned by the way galleries were "sitting on and doing nothing with" the work of his lifetime friends. In particular, he sympathized with the family of Jerome Myers. He felt strongly that Myers' works deserved far more exposure than they were enjoying.

Beginning in 1964, Kruse did agree to let selected galleries use his works in one-man shows. However, he never signed long-term representation agreements. Instead, he agreed to only one show at a time and arranged to have his works picked up when shows closed.

The first show he agreed to in this era is mentioned earlier. The Kruses good friend, David Brenner, a CPA, rented a large store at 133 East Forty-seventh Street, one of the busiest neighborhoods in New York for street traffic. Brenner, who provided income-tax preparation services at this location, came up with the idea that a Kruse show would produce prestige for his business and sales for the art works. It was an unorthodox arrangement. But at least Alex Kruse trusted Dave Brenner, which was more than he was ready to do with traditional art dealers. As described earlier, one of the clients who walked in on this show was the retired judge who had been the model for the *Young Smoker*.

Having broken the ice in this way, Kruse was ready to risk showings in "regular" galleries. When he finally agreed to traditional one-man shows, he really went into action. The year after the Brenner exhibit, 1965, Kruse was featured in a one-man show at the Carter Gallery at 900 North La Cienega Boulevard, Los Angeles.

This arrangement came about as a kind of silver lining from a cloud represented by the first serious illness in Alex Kruse's life. The Kruses in Los Angeles that winter on one of a number of trips. Ben and his family had moved to Los Angeles from Chicago for health reasons in 1954. Thereafter, and with reluctance, Alex and Anna Kruse made several cross-country trips to visit the growing family. In December of 1964, Alex and Anna were in Los Angeles for the Bar Mitzvah of their oldest grandson, Martin Alexander, when Alex suffered his first-ever stay in a hospital. Because of his prostate surgery, he missed the ceremony and also stayed on in Los Angeles longer than originally planned. During the Kruses' stay at an apartment hotel in Hollywood, Alex was introduced to Earl Carter, the gallery owner, and an exhibition was arranged. It ran from June 3 through June 25, 1965.

The show was well received critically and also enjoyed a good rate of sales. Other results also were significant. Edward G. Robinson, a noted art collector as well as actor, attended the Carter show. He and Alex recognized each other as fellow alumni from P.S. 2 on the Lower East Side and struck up a friendship that lasted the rest of their lives. A few years later, when Robinson received an honorary doctoral degree from City College of New York, his alma mater, the Kruses attended the ceremony as his personal guests.

It was also during this trip to Los Angeles that the Kruses encountered Will and Ariel Durant, renewed their friendship, and struck up the relationship described in an earlier chapter. Among the patrons who purchased paintings at the 1965 Carter show were Maria Cole, widow of Nat "King" Cole, and June Crosby, wife of Bob Crosby. June Crosby became a friend and enthusiastic fan of Kruse's work; she was the person who arranged for the final exhibition before Alex's death.

Despite the warmth of its climate and the human love he encountered, some aspects of life and work in California proved strange and hard for Alex Kruse to adjust to. One of his difficulties was with California landscapes. Family members and friends took him for long drives and visits to areas widely reputed for their beauty. But Alex remained an Easterner in his tastes for landscape.

"There's no middle ground. How can you paint a scene filled with nothing in particular?" he would ask.

The mountains are beautiful, he would agree, but they are always far away. There may be houses and things in the foreground, but then there's nothing for miles until you come to the mountains. His reaction was simply to tap his vast reserve of sketches showing his beloved Lower East Side or the countryside in Westchester or New England and paint away contentedly.

Some of the people he met in California also proved strange to his experience and sensibilities. For example, during one stay at an apartment in Tujunga, the mountain community at the edge of Los Angeles where Ben and his family resided, arrangements were made to have the local route driver who delivered seltzer and soft drinks stop by Alex and Anna's place in the course of his weekly rounds. One day, as the driver crossed the living room to make his delivery in the kitchen, he stopped to look over Alex's shoulder. The driver became irate and announced. "You're doing it all wrong." Alex looked up quizzically as the driver continued: "You've covered up all the numbers."

Other enthusiastic followers acquired by Alex Kruse during his visits to California included his three grandchildren. Liane, the oldest, showed artistic talents and shared a few painting experiences with Alex. The two boys, Martin and Steven, were frequently at his elbow when he set up his sketching outfit in their yard in Tujunga.

Alex Kruse's grandsons, Steven (left) and Martin, were an avid audience when he set up and painted on the front lawn of the Tujunga home.

No matter what attractions California offered, Alex and Anna Kruse remained New Yorkers to the core. They would journey to California when Alex suffered regular bouts of respiratory discomfort as winter set in. Then, when the weather improved, the lure of New York and of summers on nearby Fire Island proved irrestible.

The Kruses spent seven summers on Fire Island during the late 1950s and 1960s. Alex became something of a fixture, or local eccentric attraction. He would wander around the Island pulling a little red wagon (no cars are allowed on the Island) until he found a location that interested him. Then he would simply pull the wagon into position, set up a portable stool alongside and create 12" by 16" sketches in oil which he used through the fall and winter as the basis for larger paintings.

Alex enjoyed telling of an incident that occurred during one of his Fire Island painting sessions. A man who was a stranger came up behind him and watched. Then the onlooker rudely said that Alex ought to read a book that had been a great help to his wife—called *How to Draw and Paint*. The man marched off and came back with his wife. Both rather rudely looked at Alex's work and thrust the book at him. Alex took the book and tried to be civil, leafing through it so rapidly they became angered. While the man was expressing his anger at this "amateur's" behavior, Alex turned to the title page and autographed the book "Cordially, A. Z. Kruse." The wife gaped, grabbed the book, and nudged her husband. "This slob wrote that book," she said. "Let's beat it!"

After seven summers of working on Fire Island, Kruse generated a significant body of work that captured the life and activities of the seaside resort.

Ben (left) and Alex Kruse at Burrell exhibit.

Despite efforts of friends and family to entice them to stay in California following the 1965 show at the Carter Gallery, the Kruses were back in New York the following year, where Kruse was featured in a one-man show at the Burrell Gallery, 955 Madison Avenue (at Seventy-fifth Street, across the street from the Whitney Museum). This show, which ran from November 23 through December 13, was a fifty-year retrospective. Even with the New York art world still in the midst of a binge on nonrepresentational art, Kruse's exhibit, as was typical, did extremely well critically, thanks largely to his solid reputation and a high level of personal respect earned over decades of commitment to the New York art scene.

In addition to favorable reviews in print, a particularly valued reaction to the Burrell show came in a letter, dated December 6, 1966, from Virginia Myers Downes, daughter of his internationally respected friend and teacher, Jerome Myers. Mrs. Downes wrote:

> Last Saturday I had the pleasure of seeing your very fine exhibition of paintings at the Burrell Galleries…
>
> Every painting is exciting in its individual feeling. Especially I loved "Ulmer Park 1925" and "Luna Park Carousel 1930." You are a wonderful artist and it was truly a privilege to know your work.
>
> Especially in these days when so many of the modern paintings are cold and meaningless to me. I guess I still think of art in the terms of men like Jerome, you, and Sloan.

The following year, the Kruses were back in Los Angeles with a promise to stay permanently. Kruse renewed his acquaintance with Earl Carter, who opened another one-man show for Alex on February 4, 1968. This show was received even better than the previous exhibition, partly because Kruse had developed a West Coast following by then.

The "permanent" relocation lasted another year. The Kruses became restless. But they stayed for a gala celebration that encompassed their granddaughter's wedding and their youngest grandson's Bar Mitzvah over a single hectic weekend in early September, 1968. Then they were off again in the fall, giving as one of their reasons that Alex missed being able to walk down Fifty-seventh Street or Madison Avenue and recognize familiar faces.

Experience did prove that Alex Kruse was, indeed, a known quantity in his home town. From May 12 through 26, 1970, Kruse had a one-man show at the Wiener Gallery, 963 Madison Avenue, just two doors north of the Burrell Gallery, which had closed in the interim because of Eugene Burrell's health problems. Again, the show was moderately successful and provided a level of recognition that was fitting for an artist who was eighty-two years old by then and still active with undiminished power and productivity as a painter.

By the summer of 1970, even contemplation of the onset of cold weather proved too much for Alex and Anna Kruse. But, being the people they were, they still felt it necessary to call their family in California to make sure they would not be imposing if they undertook yet one more relocation. Accordingly, they called on a Saturday at the end of July to talk about the prospects. At the time, Ben was working in Detroit every other week. Since he was not home when his parents called, he reassured them with excerpts from the following letter, dated August 2, 1970, which is significant because of the way it describes the family relationships that had evolved.

> When we told the kids on Saturday that you'd called and talked to Betti, they were all over us immediately, wanting to know for sure that you're still planning to come out to stay.
> …There's so much love waiting here that I'm convinced now an irresistible force is at work. I say this for all of us. During the past few years, we've matured in our mutual understanding of each other. We can take security and satisfaction in our mutual love without doubt at this point. With security and understanding we don't each have to prove ourselves to the others. That, as the kids say, is where it's at.

By the time this final move was completed, Alex's oldest grandson, Martin, was on his own and driving. As Martin found excuses to take Alex for walks or drives in Hollywood, they became fast friends. Among their discoveries was the establishment of a Cuban cigar maker who still rolled his products by hand the way Sigmund had done ninety years earlier. Alex proved that his fabulous memory was intact by moving to the bench and rolling perfect cigars himself, the way his father had taught him.

In early 1972, the final showing of his work that Alex Kruse was able to attend was held at a small gallery, the Art and Design Center, in Bonsall, California, a plush residential area in northern San Diego County. June Crosby, who lived nearby and knew the owners, Mr. and Mrs. Hy Huling, made the introductions that led to the show, which ran from February 13 through March 5. On the days he spent in Bonsall, Kruse appeared tired. But visitors still found it fascinating to talk with him. Though he had to sit through all the conversations, lacking the stamina to stand, he showed no loss of his mental acuity.

On Sunday, March 20, 1972, Alex Kruse finished and signed his last painting, developed from sketches he had made on his honeymoon in 1923. The family still keeps the painting on the same easel where Alex left it.

That Sunday night, Anna ministered to a party of family and friends, just as she had been doing for more than forty-eight years. The following Monday, with Alex visibly fading, Anna called an ambulance which took him to a Hollywood hospital. Twelve days later—right after the start of the Passover holiday and, coincidentally on Good Friday, March 31, 1972, Alex Kruse was gone. He was buried on Easter Sunday, April 2, 1972, a religious event that also coincided with Passover. Religious friends assured the family that the coincidence of the dates with important holy days made for a good sign.

Anna Kruse lasted three more years, with her health failing gradually as she showed increasingly serious aftereffects of the heart attack she had suffered in 1962. Anna Kruse died on the morning of May 8, 1975, as she was relaxing and reading her morning newspaper before she was to embark on the day's business of cooking a dinner for Ben and Betti Kruse, who were planning to visit that evening.

Index